# GOLDEN SLUMBERS
### a novel

**DANIEL HOFFMANN**

*Bobby Mac —*
*Enjoy!*

*Golden Slumbers* is a work of fiction. References to real people, events, establishments, organizations, or locales are intended only to provide a sense of authenticity and are used fictitiously. All characters, incidents and dialogue are drawn from the authors imagination and are not to be construed as real.

Copyright © 2025 Daniel Hoffmann

All rights reserved. No part of this publication may be reproduced, stored in any retrieval system, or transmitted in any form or by any means, mechanical, photocopying, recording, or otherwise, without permission in writing from the publisher.

Book written by Daniel Hoffmann
Cover design by Daniel Hoffmann
Book layout by Rosanna Cerutti
Editing by Rebekah Icenesse


Manufactured in the United States of America

For more information, please contact:
Publishing Concepts LLC
6590 Scanlan Avenue
St. Louis, MO 63139
www.PublishingConceptsLLC.com

PAPERBACK ISBN: 978-1-957307-87-9

EBOOK (PDF) ISBN: 978-1-957307-88-6

FICTION / Coming of Age

FICTION / Beatles

1 2 3 4 5 6 7 8 9 10

**Golden Slumbers**
Words and Music by John Lennon and Paul McCartney
Copyright © 1969 Sony Music Publishing (US) LLC
Copyright Renewed
All Rights Administered by Sony Music Publishing (US) LLC, 424 Church Street, Suite 1200, Nashville, TN 37219
International Copyright Secured. All Rights Reserved
*Reprinted by Permission of Hal Leonard LLC*

**Strawberry Fields Forever**
Words and Music by John Lennon and Paul McCartney
Copyright © 1967 Sony Music Publishing (US) LLC
Copyright Renewed
All Rights Administered by Sony Music Publishing (US) LLC, 424 Church Street, Suite 1200, Nashville, TN 37219
International Copyright Secured. All Rights Reserved
*Reprinted by Permission of Hal Leonard LLC*

**Nowhere Man**
Words and Music by John Lennon and Paul McCartney
Copyright © 1965 Sony Music Publishing (US) LLC
Copyright Renewed
All Rights Administered by Sony Music Publishing (US) LLC, 424 Church Street, Suite 1200, Nashville, TN 37219
International Copyright Secured. All Rights Reserved
*Reprinted by Permission of Hal Leonard LLC*

**Two Of Us**
Words and Music by John Lennon and Paul McCartney
Copyright © 1969, 1970 Sony Music Publishing (US) LLC
Copyright Renewed
All Rights Administered by Sony Music Publishing (US) LLC, 424 Church Street, Suite 1200, Nashville, TN 37219
International Copyright Secured. All Rights Reserved
*Reprinted by Permission of Hal Leonard LLC*

**No. 9 Dream**
Words and Music by John Lennon
Copyright © 1974 (Renewed) LENONO MUSIC
All Rights Administered by DOWNTOWN DMP SONGS/DOWNTOWN MUSIC PUBLISHING LLC
All Rights Reserved   Used by Permission
*Reprinted by Permission of Hal Leonard LLC*

# GOLDEN SLUMBERS
a novel

# *Prologue*

I WAS NAÏVE THEN, at twenty-two, living my simple reality at odds with my surroundings—the Los Angeles of beaches, billboards, big dreams, backdoor schemes, and *black magic*.

Barely a year later and I'd changed—forever, not for better. I'd come into possession of something that wasn't meant for me—a ruinous something that showed me two hard truths: one—there are dark forces at work in the world that you and I aren't meant to know, and two—there's a girl within reach that I'm not meant to have.

This is my story. When it's over, I will have told you everything—just as it happened to me. And it will be yours to decide whether to believe me. Living is easy with eyes closed, misunderstanding all you see. Isn't that how John said it—in his song—"Strawberry Fields"?

Every story has its beginning. I guess mine began when I met Tommy. Tommy Scanlon and I went to the same high school—Hollywood High. In our class of '74, there were two other Jeffs: Jeff Butterfield—a real brainiac and faculty favorite, and then there was this aspiring actor who insisted on being called *Geoffrey*. We all, save a few ducky girls, did the *actor* a service and just called him *Plain Jeff*. So, with two other Jeffs, everyone called me *Walk*, which was good by me. My name's Jeff Scott Walker. Four years of high school and no great adventures to speak of. My adventure was to come later.

But already, I'm getting ahead of myself.

## Chapter One

I RODE MY YAMAHA up into the hills, up streets lined with a continuous chain of adobe walls smothered in restless ivy and red bougainvillea. Methodically, an opening—a sleek teak or iron gate—behind which rich people hid in their rich people houses.

When I ran out of street, I parked my bike in a concealed spot, jammed my lunch bag into the pocket of my cords and set out on foot through steep fields of dry grass battered with stone outcroppings. At the trail's end, I pulled back a loose section of chain link fence and squeezed past the posted *no trespassing* sign.

It was the morning of my junior mid-terms and mine wouldn't be the only empty seat—not if Tommy's plan played out. Tommy had hatched the idea just the day prior, sharing it with me and an unknown few. "You know we have tests tomorrow," I told him.

"I know. It's perfect," he grinned. It really wasn't like me to ditch school, but I didn't want to disappoint Tommy.

According to the plan, everyone was to meet at the prescribed location by 8:30 a.m.—"Weed to be provided."

Mid-way to the summit, the low grass gave way to scrub oaks that, at times, obscured my view of the hilltop destination, the sun glinting off its giant sprawling letters. I stood at the foot of the iconic structure, hands on hips, to catch my breath and have a look around. I was the first to arrive. I scaled the legs of the W and perched there, surveying the hills below expecting to see Tommy and the others on their ascent. There was no sign of them. I checked my watch—8:47.

Minutes passed, then an hour—time spent climbing the sign scaffolding and hurling rocks at makeshift targets. Checking my watch again, it was 10:14. I sat with my back against the D and felt its warmth penetrate my shirt. I thought about my teachers, the missed tests, my grades. I tried to convince myself none of it mattered. It's not like I'd studied anyway. I was always one to do just the bare minimum—to just wing it. While my grades I could push aside, I couldn't chase off the kick in the gut that rankled my insides. I couldn't let go of being played for the fool. My escalating anger found a voice in choice words that echoed down the hillside—*asshole, stupid fucker, stupid fucking asshole*—all directed at my so-called friend.

All that screaming made me hungry. I pried my lunch from the car wreck of a bag. The bread was pressed gooey and transparent against the flat meat inside where my tangerine made its crater. I ate the tangerine first. My smashed sandwich went down in two big swallows. The bag of chips was relieved of its air—only salty crumbs remained. I held the bag to my mouth and poured the last of it past my lips. Thirst bit into my throat and I knew it was time to give it up. My watch read 11:06.

Back on my feet, my eyes caught something moving in the distance. I squinted into the sun. Someone was coming—it was Tommy—Tommy and a girl. I stood my ground until they were within fifteen feet—close enough to see the smart-ass smirk on Tommy's face. Something snapped inside of me and I rushed him, knocking him to the ground—me on top wailing away with balled fists. I was hit with a force at my side and found myself on my back—someone on top grasping my arms and holding them down. It was the girl. She was screaming, "Leave him alone, leave him alone."

I screamed back, angry spit spraying from my words, "Get off me!" I jerked my arms free, but she found my wrists again with her adrenaline-charged grip. I stopped struggling and looked at her face. I laid there, taking her in, and heard myself say, calmly this time, "Get off of me."

Tommy stood over the two of us, beating dried grass from his backside and grinning that fucking grin of his. "Walk, meet Jules. Jules, this here is Walk."


TOMMY WAS ALL ABOUT LOYALTY. He'd test me often as he did that day I first met Jules under the Hollywood sign. It was, as I told you, a disastrous introduction, but Tommy was quite sure he had the remedy in the form of a bag of reefers— "A smorgasbord of the exotic," he called it. We three found a spot on the dried grass beneath the neglected sign. Jules and I followed Tommy's lead by sitting cross-legged in a tight circle. Tommy held up the bag to Jules and offered, "Lady's choice." She pointed to a monstrously fat one. "An excellent selection," he grinned. When she asked what variety it was, he smiled his fabrication, "Katmandu." He put a flame to its tightly rolled tip and a bitter scent shook loose. He took a long drag—*don't mind if I do*—and passed it to Jules. She first fingered it like you would a cigarette, held it at arm's length for a good look, then adjusted her grip to a classic pinch. She took a tight puff, flashed a smile, and passed it to me. I took my first hit ever—*it stung*—and passed it on.

Tommy—Jules—me. Tommy—Jules—me. The monster floated from Tommy's lips to Jules' lips, to mine. We went around like that, keeping expectant watch over each other's faces, convinced we'd witness some sort of transformation. What does *high* look like anyway?

It felt intimate, sitting so close and staring so deeply. Normally, you'd get called a freak for staring at a girl like that. Jules was hard to take your eyes off. She had an energy about her that to look away meant you'd miss something. Her hair was a soft brown and beyond her shoulders—a slight widow's peak at the part just off center of her forehead. She'd work her hair non-stop by raking it back with spread fingers. Her eyes—liquid brown, long lashes, framed by thick expressive brows. Her nose was what I'd call elegant but had a cute quality too, and she crinkled it often. Her lips plumped when they held the reefer and otherwise were mostly being bitten at the corners. I saw Tommy studying her too, both of us entranced, both expecting her pot-fueled transformation into the girl with kaleidoscope eyes. But that day, her baby browns revealed only a glimpse of Jules' hippie essence we would come to know.

"My throat," Jules said, her voice huskier now. She reached for her backpack and dug out a can of Coca-Cola. She held it up for us to see—*found treasure*. She pulled the tab and took a micro sip. "Warm," she smiled and used both hands to pass it to me. I took a little more than a sip and held the fizz in my mouth before sending it down my raw throat.

Meanwhile, Tommy lit up again. "Panama Red," he called that one. He had no idea.

As the Coke became part of our rotation, Jules would remind us with each turn—"Tiny sips." When that proved to be not enough of a deterrent, she took to keeping hold of the can as Tommy or I brought it to our mouths. She'd pull the can away saying—"Let go"—but it came out *leggo*.

"Leggo-leggo," she'd say excitedly as we clung on. If I'm being honest, for me it became not about another sip, but the feel of her warm hands wrapped around mine. As her policing turned comical, Tommy spouted, "You can Bogart my toke but never her Coke." We laughed, but not as hard as Tommy—*at his own joke*—which made it all the funnier. When the roach came to me next, I took a long pull and, on my exhale, let "Leggo" ride the wave of smoke exiting the side of my mouth. Jules read this as the tease intended and began to rise up until I added, "—my Eggo."

"Leggo-my-Eggo!" I grinned.

Tommy, who was having his turn with the Coke, lost it. He spilled the precious little left in the can which prompted Jules to turn her killing spree on him.

When their tussle ended, Tommy sat up with a crazed look in his eyes and said, "I'm hungry—for frozen waffles."

We three set out down the hillside for the nearest 7-Eleven on our grand quest for the golden box with the loopy, red-letter logo. The weed erased the small problem of how we were going to toast the waffles once we had them. Along the way someone started in with the rhymes—

"Leggo-my-Eggo, Bucko."

"You Leggo-my-Eggo. Comprendo?"

"No. You Leggo-my-Eggo, Muchacho."

"—Vincenzo."

"—Fucko."

"—Prego."

"God, No!"

ULTIMATELY, WE NEVER MADE it to the 7-Eleven.

The house break-ins were Tommy's idea. He went into the first house alone and came busting out with a stolen bottle of syrup but was laughing so hard he fumbled it on the driveway. I don't know why a shattered bottle of syrup was so funny—it just was.

Soon we were all three entering through unlocked doors. Being where I didn't belong was a rush—the unknown breathing down my neck and the unfamiliar rooms whispering—*you're not supposed to be here*. It was a feeling I'd come to know too well.

Jules was so funny. She'd tiptoe around the entire time in the houses, like that made it okay to be invading someone's home.

Apparently, nobody kept frozen waffles in their freezers.

"What's wrong with these people?" Tommy kept saying.

We were hungry enough—high enough—to seriously consider making pancakes at one house. When Tommy pulled a loaf of bread from a pantry with a gleam in his eye, we settled on toast. I opened the fridge and extracted a tub of Oleo. Tommy rejected that straight away and dug until he found a new stick of Land-O-Lakes. Checking that Jules wasn't looking, Tommy chugged from a juice carton and tossed it to me like a hot potato. I swallowed the last of it and put it back in the door empty.

Jules commandeered the toaster—convinced us boys would either bust it or burn the place down.

The way I remember it, toast never tasted so good—at the forbidden kitchen table—the three of us. It was seriously the best time of my life.

Jules insisted we pay for what we ate. Tommy wrote—*Toast Good*—and drew a cartoon caveman on a dollar bill. I added—*Best*—but wrote it left-handed so a court-appointed handwriting expert couldn't tag me. As for Jules? She drew a peace sign on the one-spot before leaving it there next to the toaster and tiptoeing out.

Tommy borrowed my Yamaha to take Jules home. Once again, I was left alone to wait, to wonder. But Tommy came back. Tommy came back grinning from ear-to-ear—said he was "in love."

*Yeah, right.* Taking note of his black eye and busted lip, I apologized for jumping him earlier.

"No sweat," he smiled, "but next time I'll be swinging back."


A FRUSTRATED TEACHER ONCE asked Tommy what he intended to be when he graduated high school. "Not a day over eighteen," was his reply. That was Tommy Scanlon—singular, certain. There was nobody else like him. Not in my orbit anyway.

Actually, Tommy was the first to call me Walk. It was junior year and I was in my usual spot standing among the fringe crowd while sides were being chosen in gym class. Tommy knew me—*of me*—but we never really hung out or exchanged more than a hallway head nod.

"Walk!" Tommy called out loudly so that everyone would know his first choice. He then grabbed me around my neck and pulled me in. He said just to me, "Comrades."

I played out of my mind that day and Tommy's team won the softball game. That was it—our beginning. The name stuck and lucky for me so did the friendship.

We *comrades* were an unlikely pair. Him, the All-American—blonde hair, green eyes, movie star features and a decathlete's body. Tommy excelled in sports—lighting it up in gym class. But you know, Tommy out-and-out refused to play on any school team—drove all the coaches mad. He'd give them no reason. "Not my thing is all."

As for me? Call me All-Average—average height, average weight, average grades, average athlete. I had a decent arm though—made varsity baseball my sophomore year. And I guess you could say I had average looks—lurking somewhere beneath all that enraged acne.

Like I said—an unlikely pair. I was the quiet straight man to his funny man, the tame Beach Boy to his Johnny Rotten, and yes, sadly, the pizza face to his picture-perfect face. Sometimes, I thought maybe he kept me around for that contrast. But Tommy was good to me—he really was. Tommy had access to a car, and I didn't. He'd pick me up and we'd go cruising. We would hit the fast-food joints and he almost always paid. We spent a lot of time at his Uncle Steve's place—a huge house with both a pool and pool table, not to mention a fridge just for beer.

Another plus to being tight with Tommy was the girls. He'd attract them and I'd hope to land one for myself from his overflow. They'd circle, waiting for their shot at Tommy, and I'd—well, I'd keep them company. Always a friend, nothing more.

The parade of girls ended when Jules came along. Julia Helene Nichols transferred into Hollywood High mid-way through our junior year and marched right to the center of our world that day under the Hollywood sign. Tommy would never be the same, and honestly, neither would I.

## WALKER RESIDENCE/LOS ANGELES/SEPTEMBER 1973

Caroline Walker held the telephone to her ear with her shoulder, a can of spray cleaner in one hand and a towel rag in the other. She listened.

"Can I talk to the boy?"
"He's in the shower."
"Oh—okay."
"No, I'll get him. He's been in there forever. He's going to scrub the skin right off his face."
"No. Let him be."
"No. I'll get him. The water's got to be ice-cold by now."
"No, don't. Let him be."

Caroline stretched the phone cord around the corner into the hall toward the bathroom. "Poor kid, I mean, it just keeps getting worse," she said, turning around after realizing the phone cord wouldn't reach.

"Did you get him some of that stuff, that cream?"
"He won't use it, says it stinks."
"Does it?"
"Yeah, it kinda does."
Silence.

"Well, I have to go. Will you please tell him I called?"
"Of course. Why wouldn't I?"
"I didn't mean it like that."
"How did you mean it, Scott?"

Silence.

"Caroline, I'm gonna go."
"Yeah—okay—sure. It's what you do."

Stinging, Caroline Walker hung up the phone. She sprayed a heavy cover of cleaner on the already clean counter. Later, false-heartedly chipper, she'd tell her son, Jeff, that his father had called.

## Chapter Two

Not long after our first toaster session in that stranger's Hollywood Hills kitchen, the three of us went out to the Strand—Topanga State Beach south of Malibu. It's a little over an hour's drive. Tommy drove a loaner Benz 280 from his Uncle Steve's dealership. He'd strapped two boards to the roof, the cords wound through the open windows. Jules sat shotgun and I centered myself in the back leaning forward between them. Jules' hair kept whipping into my face. She'd say sorry and pull it back tight behind her head, but it wouldn't stay put. As soon as she'd let go, it'd blow right back. I didn't mind. Her hair smelled good—like rain.

We practically had to yell to hear each other over the wind coming in the windows and Tommy blaring KROQ. Tommy was in his own world, guitar strumming the wheel and singing about your *China Grove*. He was winging most the verses, but he had the chorus and guitar licks down cold. As Tommy occupied himself with his tunes, Jules and I made conversation.

"Walk, been to Topanga?"
"Huh?—oh—yeah."
"It's beautiful, isn't it?"
"What?"
"I said the coast is pretty there."
"Yeah—very pretty—best."
"Do you surf?"
"Huh? Oh. No. Never tried it."
"Maybe today?"
"Huh?"
"Maybe you'll try today."
"Uh—Yeah—maybe."
"I hear Tommy's really good," she yelled putting her hand on his forearm. "So he says."

Tommy let go of the wheel and thrust his two fists forward in self-adulation.

I nodded my head, yes. *I'd figured.* "How about you? Bet you're good."

"Not too bad," she smiled. "But I can always get better."

"For sure," I said. "I mean, the more you do it, right?"

I learned some about Jules on that ride. She's the baby—two older sisters, Liz and Trudy. Jules was her dad's last chance for a boy. I'm glad for his disappointment. They'd moved from San Luis Obispo for her dad's new job—logistics or something.

I didn't share much of anything about me. "Not much to tell," I told her. "No brothers or sisters. Live with my mom. Dad lives in Oregon."

"Sorry," she said.

"Huh?"

"Your parents—divorced?"

"Not officially, but yeah."

"Where in Oregon?"

"Bend."

"See him much?"

"Nah."

"That sucks."

"Yeah. I guess."


Tommy and Jules pulled on their wetsuits at the trunk of the car while I unraveled the boards. They both let their top halves hang at the waist for the walk to the beach. Jules had on a tangerine orange string bikini top. It looked so good against her skin.

We planted the boards in the sand to mark our spot and Tommy led the charge into the surf—them in their skin suits and me in my shorts. Damn, the water was cold. Tommy apologized again for not having an extra skin for me. He offered me his over and over on the ride, but I declined. Out in the water, we treaded neck deep, facing the shoreline for a time—smiling at each other but not saying much. Jules submerged and resurfaced about twenty feet away. She then freestyled it out another twenty or so.

"What do you think?" Tommy grinned.

"She's great," I said, teeth chattering. "Really sweet."

"Rockin' that bikini," he said.

"Best."

Jules had U-turned and was heading back our way.

"Think I'll go spear me a mermaid," he said.

"I'll leave you to it," I said, and turned toward dry land.

I dunked my head multiple times on the way into shore. I'd heard salt water was good for acne—dries it up. *Salt water and maybe a good sandblasting might do the trick.* I scooped a handful of moving sand, felt its grit between my fingers, and actually considered it.

From the beach, I watched them bobbing in unison like two seals in a mating dance. I couldn't help but feeling I wished I'd seen her first—but who was I kidding. Anyway, I was happy for Tommy. I think he really liked her—and not the way he liked those other girls. I was laying back in the sand drying my face when they came in for the boards. I raised my head slightly, squinting at them standing over me. "Watch us," Jules smiled.

They paddled out and waited. Jules was first to catch one. She popped right up and rode it out until the board stalled beneath her, then stepped off into the foam. Tommy caught a bigger one and cut his board back into the curl. He hung on for a bit but then chose to abort by diving head-first into the crumbling wave. After maybe a dozen rides, they seemed to have had enough and were content to just sit their boards out beyond the waves.

I was sitting up, eyeing the beach walkers and the occasional runaway dog, when they finally came in. Tommy lent his shoulder to Jules as she peeled off her wetsuit. I looked away when she nearly lost her bikini bottoms in the process. "Sorry," she said, pulling them back in place and then slipping on a pair of cut-offs from her bag. *There was no sorry about it.*

Jules' legs were athletic. She had that little roll of muscle above her knees when she stood relaxed. As Jules turned away to straighten her orange top, I stole glances of her tan lines—sculpted caramel teasing creamy curves. *Damn!*

Tommy tried to pretend he wasn't looking too. He stepped out of his wetsuit and held it out to me. "Your turn," he said.

"Uh?"

"He needs a lesson first," Jules said.

"Have at it," Tommy said, and laid the long boards out side-by-side in the sand.

Jules grabbed my arm and pulled me upright. "Watch closely and do as I do," she instructed. She laid belly-down on the board. I did the same. She demonstrated the paddle out with her arms. I paddled my arms the same way. "Grip the board with the balls of your feet—spread your toes—that's it—you got it!"

ON THE WAY HOME, Stealers Wheel came on the radio and we all three belted out "Stuck In The Middle With You". Jules did this thing where she'd turn down the volume so it would just be our voices. She was trying to catch us messing up the lyrics or singing off-key. Tommy was doing a lot of both—on purpose.

When "Ramblin' Man" came on, Jules got all excited and began bouncing in her seat—said it was her favorite song. Tommy and I started singing along and she swatted at us to stop—said she wanted to hear Gregg Allman—said she loved him. *I wasn't going to be the one to tell her that Dickey Betts sings lead on that Allman Brothers' song.*

Anyway, of course Tommy and I kept at it. Tommy took to playing her game by jerking down the volume in spots. Jules twisted the pinky finger on his hand, but he would no way let loose of that knob. He was laughing too hard to sing so I carried on solo. As she batted away at me to stop, I bobbed and weaved in the backseat, singing all the while. When Tommy turned down the volume and held it there, Jules stopped swinging. She turned her head toward me in the back, resting her chin on the bench seat—listening, watching me. Tommy brought the volume back up as the song shifted into its long instrumental end.

When the song finally ended, Jules said to me, "You're pretty darn good, Bucko. But I'll always love Gregg." *Dickey.*

At that, Tommy clutched at his heart.

Jules said to him, "Like that thing could ever be broken." Then she lunged and kissed his cheek saying, "But I'm thinkin' I might have a crack at it."

AFTER THAT SATURDAY on the Strand, Tommy and Jules became official I guess—the Homecoming King and the New Girl.

I worried what their relationship would spell for me. Would Tommy's friendship and my brush with popularity come to a crushing end? But Tommy never faltered and Jules—well, she saw us as a package deal. She would never think of breaking us apart. I guess we were an entertaining pair. I liked to think that she shared Tommy with me, and from day one, I shared his love for her.

One day, at my locker, Jules jumped my back. Her arms clinging needy around my neck, she pleaded, "Walk! Walk! Where's Tommy?"

I continued business as usual in my locker, pretending not to notice the crazy person on my back.

"Walk. Walk. Do you hear me? Where's Tommy? Where's T?"

I pushed my locker shut and spun around, still acting as if she wasn't there. I pried free her fingers on one hand, slipped my backpack strap underneath, and closed her fingers around it. I started down the crowded hall.

She wrapped her legs tight around my waist. "That's it, boy. Go find him. I need my T. Got to have my T. Must have my Vitamin T."

She rode me like that—galloped me down the halls looking for her *Vitamin T*.

He found us. We were impossible to miss. Tommy wrapped her up from behind—me included—and proceeded to run me face-first into people, mostly girls, and eventually into walls. Jules was laughing hysterically all the while. We had that effect on her.

## Chapter Three

I'D MADE A PACT with myself back in high school to never get up from a chair or out of bed without doing twenty-five push-ups and twenty-five sit-ups. I made that pact after dressing out for gym class that first time freshman year. Some guys—like Tommy—were naturally built. Me—being naturally scrawny—I realized I'd have to work at it. So, between classes, watching TV, or in my bedroom, I'd knock off my reps. By sophomore year, I was up to one hundred reps. I'd developed the broad chest and shoulders, the cut abs. Not that it mattered any. Not with the landmines going off on my face.

Thinking back, there were so many times I'd watch as Jules would pull Tommy in by his sleeve—back to her—sometimes for a kiss or to whisper something. But more often, it seemed she did it just so he'd know—so he'd know that she loved him and wanted him.

I see now that I wanted that too.

But back then—to have something of my own—a girl like Jules—it just wasn't in the cards for me. *A guy could dream though.* At least I had my baseball. I was pretty good. I made the team and that would be enough. Except even that wouldn't last.

ONCE BEFORE PRACTICE, I saw Jules and a couple of girls hanging out on the bleachers. I pulled my cap down tight over my eyes and watched her as our center fielder, Mick, and I extended our warm-up by launching long balls in the outfield. As you'd expect, the girls' presence attracted some attention from our bench. I watched as a few players moseyed over. *Clowns.* The guys goofed and of course the girls laughed. Jules too—I could hear her. This went on for a while and then Jules was gone. I motioned quits to Mick and jogged in. I saw Jules on the side of the gym but I couldn't see who she was with. I walked to the fountain to get closer—took a long slurp. I heard them talking—flirting and shit. Then I saw him kiss her. And the thing is—she didn't push away. They came skipping out of there and I turned away. But I saw him. I saw who it was.

A WEEK PASSED. I lifted the arm of the stylus from my record mid-song and left my room. Back in high school, I had a sixth sense for when there were fresh groceries in the house. I found my mom in the kitchen unloading paper bags that crowded the counter. I began to scavenge through the goods without so much as a hello.

"I like that song," she said, "—what you were just listening to."

"Huh? Oh, yeah—Cat Stevens."

"La-la-la-la on a moon shadow," she sang.

"Ice cream?" I asked.

"Not until we finish the old."

I mumbled something for her benefit about crappy Neapolitan as I uncovered a bunch of bananas and tore off a riper one.

"Practice canceled?" she asked.

"No."

She waited for more that I wasn't offering. "Not like you to skip," she said. "You feel okay?"

"I'm dandy—just not playing baseball anymore."

Mom stopped cold, a can of soup in each hand. "Then you're certainly not okay—you love your baseball."

"I'm off the team—kicked off."

"No—by who? What for?"

"By Coach—for hitting our star player with a pitch."

"That's no reason—a wild pitch. Who was it?"

"Cody."

"The Vale boy? Is he okay?"

"Not unless you consider a fractured jaw okay."

"My God. But still—a wild pitch—that's not your fault."

I dropped my banana peel in the trash and filled a glass of water at the sink.

"It wasn't your fault, right? It's not like you did it on purpose."

I finished a swallow. "I did it on purpose."

"Why? Why on earth?"

"I needed to—for loyalty's sake, let's say."

"Loyalty to who?"

"Doesn't matter."

"I'd say it matters. What do you plan on telling your father?"

"I'm not telling him anything. Since when does he care what I do?"

"He cares about your baseball." Mom grimaced as she realized how that must've sounded.

*It didn't faze me any—par for the course.*

"News to me," I said. "Last I checked, he left us—never calls."

"He would," she said. "He's just busy."

"Why do you always defend him?"

"I don't."

"Yes—you do."

"He'll call—you watch, and you'd better have your story straight."

"I don't owe anyone an explanation, least of all him." I put my empty glass in the sink and headed toward the door.

"Where are you going now?"

"Tommy's."

"Wear your helmet," she called.

But I was already gone.

I WAS WITH TOMMY when he asked Jules to prom. He took a knee right there in the school hallway and pulled me down with him. Jules, in turn, smiled down upon us and said, "Doubly Yes." So we both took her to the dance—she with two dates in matching maroon tuxes with beige trim. *Frick and Frack*, she called us.

We showed up at her home together in rented shoes, offering equally clumsy crumbling corsages. We met her mom—a real beauty, and her dad. *I swear he liked me more than Tommy*. Jules being Jules, she chose not to wear the formal dress and heels as was customary. She came down the stairs in yellow bell-bottoms with red high-tops and a flowy hippie blouse laced in front. A braided leather headband held her hair up and pulled back from her face. She plucked a poppy from my corsage and put it in her hair. She was—something. *Best.*

At the gym door, the student counselor, Mrs. Piglowski—*I kid you not*, was not going to let Jules in. But Tommy turned on the charm and the gates to adolescent mayhem magically opened to us.

Tommy took the slow dances and I the fast. He held Jules close to Chicago Transit Authority's "Colour My World" and Croce's "Time In A Bottle". I played the frolicking fool, cummerbund wrapped around my head, dancing with her to Kool's "Jungle Boogie" and Elton's "Bennie And The Jets".

Plain Jeff—*Geoffrey*, put on a choreographed performance of Redbone's "Come And Get Your Love" with the varsity cheerleaders as his Indian backup singers. It was a riot. I had to give it to him—the guy had moves.

When the balloons dropped, couples kissed and milled around the sticky hardwoods hugging their summer goodbyes. Wading through the sea of balloons and solo cups, Jules somehow found me sitting alone on the edge of the stage.

"You okay, Bucko?" she said, her hands on my knees, her eyes searching mine.

"Yeah, of course. Best."

She smiled and raised up on her tiptoes to kiss my cheek, but I flinched, and she missed. I got down and she gave me a hug.

WE THREE FOLLOWED the hungry mob to Ernie's Pancake Palace. There we huddled into our own private booth and ordered toast instead of pancakes. "Toast?" the waiter dude questioned. He looked even more the dumbshit when Tommy asked him to bring us a "thingy of syrup."

We played WTLB—words to live by.

Jules led off by saying—and I'll never forget—*Best Friends, Full Hearts, Time of our Lives.*

I followed with something lame like—*Warm Toast, Cold Butter, Let's Eat.*

And Tommy's words to live by—*Hold Your Fire,* said with both hands up and accompanied by a trigger pull on a finger pistol.

"It's not supposed to be literal," Jules said. "It's not like you're staring death in the face or something."

"Is that right?" Tommy said. "In that case, I change mine to —*Hold Your Fire,*" he said while clutching the proverbial eternal flame in his chest.

"You're impossible," Jules told him. Then she took his face in her hands and kissed him properly. I could only watch.

Outside in the parking lot, Tommy ceremoniously smashed the glass thingy of syrup on the pavement. It was nearly but not quite as funny as that first time. We three did a quickie rain dance and then ran for our lives, laughing all the way.

ONCE FOR A FULL week, Jules wore my varsity jacket. It didn't mean anything—it was all part of a joke.

Jules speared a gooey chunk of cafeteria mac and cheese and paused with the fork circling her mouth, the way she did. She said, "What I want for my birthday, huh? And it can be anything?"

"Anything," Tommy said. "Name it and it's yours."

I smiled looking on.

"But it's not even my birthday—not really. I don't have a birthday for another year."

Jules was born on February 29—a leap year baby. Just one more thing that made her special and unlike the rest of us mortals.

"Quit stalling," Tommy said to her.

"Hey—nobody's stalling. It's just that I already have everything a girl could possibly want."

"Like what? And don't say me."

"Okay—Walk then. I'll have Walk. So there!"

"Walk don't count. He's just—well, you know—Walk."

"Hey thanks, friend. Best. You're no prize yourself."

"Enough," Jules interrupted. "I love both my boys—just in different ways."

Tommy said, "Oh yeah? I wasn't aware I was sharing you. I don't take too kindly to sharing."

I said, "Back on point, people—the bell's about to ring."

"Right you are, Walk. Jules—the time has come. Speak now or expect a chocolate bar and pantyhose for your birthday."

I smiled at Tommy's reference to what we were just learning in history class—WWII German-occupied France.

Jules' eyes tracked Christina Hart as she passed by. "I want one of those," she pointed.

Tommy followed Christina's wiggle across the room. "What? You want a three-way?"

I laughed.

"Not the girl—you big dummy—the jacket. I want to wear my boyfriend's letter jacket like every other respectable girl around here."

"No can do," Tommy said.

"You said anything—anything at all—name it and it's yours, you said."

"But I don't have a letter jacket to give you. You know that."

"Not my problem," Jules said.

"Walk," Tommy said, "—stand up."

I did.

"Take it off."

I slid out of my varsity jacket and handed it over.

Tommy moved behind Jules' chair. "Now, you stand." She did. Tommy slipped my jacket on her. "Done," he said. "Saved me the wrapping."

Jules looked at me. I nodded. "Sure?" she smiled.

"Sure," I smiled back.

Jules clutched at my oversized jacket, pulling it closed across her chest. She addressed both Tommy and me—curtsied, smiled, and curtsied again just as the lunch bell rang. She picked up her fork and stabbed one last bite of macaroni. Chewing, she pointed at me as she was leaving. "To be continued," she said.

Tommy did get Jules a real present—silver and turquoise earrings. She loved them. Still, she wore my jacket out to her birthday dinner with Tommy. That's what he told me anyway—joked that every time he went to kiss her, he'd get a whiff of me and had to abort. He also told me that they did it on top of the jacket and that I might want to get it cleaned.

Days later, Jules came to me in the hall holding my folded jacket in her outstretched arms. "It was fun while it lasted," she said. "You're sweet."

"You sure?" I said, "you can keep it."

"No. It's yours. You need it."

"I don't—that's the thing. I'm off the team."

"You are not—since when?"

"Since Coach canned me."

"Canned you? For what?"

"Beaning a guy with a pitch."

Jules' face went pale. "Who? Who did you hit?"

I didn't answer.

She pushed me into an open classroom. "Cody? Was it Cody?"

I held my silence. In her eyes, I saw she had her answer.

"What did you see?" she pleaded. "Walk, tell me—*please.*"

All I said was, "He had it coming."

"Oh, Walk—NO. Whatever you saw—it wasn't like that."

"He put the move on you."

"No. He didn't—I mean—yeah, he kissed me—but."

"But what? The guy's a slime ball."

"Walk—listen—oh shit. Walk—I asked him. I asked him to. It was innocent—you know—flirting—just being silly. I called his bluff—it was me."

"I know that part. I saw. He's still a slime ball."

"You saw? You knew and you didn't tell Tommy?"

Jules held me—my jacket between us—held me a long time. She said she was sorry—for getting me kicked off the team—for everything. She pulled away and wiped at her eyes. "Thank you, Walk," she whispered.

*No thanks necessary really. Being held by Jules like that seemed worth getting kicked off the baseball team.*

Thanksgiving that year, Tommy and I were invited to Jules' parents' home—a chance to see the Nichols again, Norah and Walt. Even better that Jules' two sisters were coming, husbands in tow.

Middle sister, Trudy, greeted T and me at the door. "Well, if it isn't Frick and Frack," she said, "which one's which?"

"Walk," I said, raising my hand.

"Frick," Tommy said, raising his.

To see the sisters together in one place it was obvious—they got prettier on down. All beauties for sure, but baby Jules took the cake.

The family was like their own social club—the three girls of course—but mom and dad too. They spoke their own shorthand and shared quirky rituals. They even shared the same eye rolls—doled out liberally. Only their laughs were unique— though one couldn't go without the others joining in.

Trudy went one year to Boston College, met Kurt, dropped out, and married him. They live in Worcester. Kurt manages rental property and Trudy works in a flower shop. Trudy is a riot and Kurt is super cool. I liked them best as a couple.

The eldest by two years, Elizabeth or Liz, of course had to be married first. So she grabbed the nearest guy and rushed into it. That's pretty much all you need to know about her Barry. Liz works as a full-time stay-at-home to her accountant husband. They live "somewhere near" San Diego.

The girls all pitched in with Norah in the kitchen—a blur of measuring, mixing, kneading, chopping, blending, browning, basting, and baking. Jules looked so cute in her apron. In perfect synchronization, they summoned a magnificent turkey and all the fixings, including yeast-raised dinner rolls and stuffing with bits of apples and raisins in it. Liz made Barry a separate dish all his own. What's the guy got against raisins?

When it came time to carve the turkey, Walt asked me to assist. Kurt told me that I must be special because not just anybody gets chosen to assist Walt-the-Butcher. Jules excitedly tied her apron around my waist. I figured I'd just stand by and watch so I was shocked, and a bit nervous, when Walt handed me the knife.

At my side, Walt instructed me in the knife sharpening while reciting the edict—*more accidents happen with dull knifes than with sharp ones*. He officiated the ceremonial first cut of the bird's crispy skin to go to Norah. Jules' mom fingered the juicy tidbit from the tip of my extended knife and said to me smiling, "You're an interesting character, aren't you?"

Walt guided me to remove the wings first, followed by the legs. My knife somehow magically found the sweet spots and the joints separated trouble free. Walt then had me remove both breasts to be placed on a cutting board where they could be sliced "clean and even." With the platter piled high, Walt reclaimed his treasured knife and gave me a fatherly pat on the back. *Well done*.

During the meal, the family code words had me guessing. Milk was of course—

*cow*, and turkey—*bird*. But other words were not as obvious. Gravy was *navy*, but not for the rhyme—rather, gravy boat. Salt and Pepper were *Mort and Mac*—short for the Morton's and McCormick's brand names. Chair was *duffer*—because of course you sit on your duff. "Pull over a duffer and take a load off."

Yes, great or anything in the affirmative was—*that nice*. And instead of no, they'd say—*that ain't it*. Apparently, the girls picked up the slang from a plumber making a house call when they were young and impressionable. Despite Norah's efforts to squelch it, it stuck. Even dad couldn't be housebroken.

"Walter-dear, would you like some more stuffing?"

"That nice."

"Trudy, are you planning to re-enroll in school next spring?"

"That ain't it."

After we'd finished eating, Walt and Norah banned us all from the kitchen so they alone could clean up. Trudy told me that I should be glad to have been spared the couple's bump and grind kitchen routine. So us *kids* camped out in front of the football game—Liz right at Barry's side for foot rubs and refills. The guy said "aces" when she brought him an antacid. He couldn't have said—*that nice*—like the rest of us?

During the game, the sisters would protest rulings and call the ref a *foke*. I thought they were saying fuck. "Can you spell that for me?" I asked. F-O-C, I was told—for bifocals, as in needing glasses. "Get with the program, Bucko."

When Tommy and Jules left for a walk, Trudy grabbed my arm and drug me out to the backyard saying, "Don't make me smoke alone."

On the back porch, I noticed that, in profile, she and Jules had the same nose.

Snuffing out her first butt, she asked me, "So how long?"

"Sorry," I smiled, "you're going to have to give me more than that. I don't yet speak fluent Nichol-*ese*."

"You bet," she said. "I'm asking you, Jeff Walker, how long have you loved my sister?"

I didn't answer her—just stared off beyond the fence into the quiet of the neighbor's yard.

"Thought so," she said.

Driving home with Jules between Tommy and me, I kept replaying Trudy's question. Not the—*how long?*—but the one at the door—*so which one's which?*

Did she really think that either of us could have been Jules' boyfriend?

## Chapter Four

I LIKE THE SMELL of the garage—the rubber tires, new grease and oil, the detergent of the hand cleaner. I like the sound of my scuffling work boots and the squeal of the new tires on the sealed concrete floors, the sound of tools clanking into trays, and the torque of a lone lug nut drill. I like the feel of my gray uniform—worn soft on my thighs, the tightness of my sleeves rolled up on my forearms, the slight scratch of the embroidered name patch against my chest.

Tommy and I started at his Uncle Steve's dealership the summer we graduated high school. Uncle Steve wanted to bring Tommy into the business. He had no kids of his own and poured his ambition on Tommy. As for me? Well—once again, we were a package deal.

It was a great place to work. We got our share of Hollywood celebs and hot shot businessmen. Tommy called the clientele "the Plastics" but pronounced it like the French, *les Plastiques*. It was our private little thing, like the way he'd rate the ladies on a scale of one to ten. For me—not a one of them could ever compare to Jules.

Tommy apprenticed under Tony—the *horndog*, and I was assigned the resident old guy, Gil—*the pill*. Gil lightened up when I took to it like a duck to water and I even got a smile or two out of him whenever he'd hover and I'd say to him, "Chill Gil." The day I got my certification patch, I found a new ratchet set sitting by my tools. Gil would never admit it, but I knew it was from him.

One evening, after we'd first started, Tommy and I had beers down in the garage pit. We clanked wrenches and made the mechanics pledge to live the simple life, work with our hands—*off at four and leave it at the door*. A year-to-the-day later, Tommy came to work wearing a crisp white shirt and a big ol' smile. Service Manager—he was on his way. Jules used to tell us we looked good in charcoal gray. She couldn't say that about Tommy anymore.

Tommy's promotion didn't change a thing between us though. With his raise, he moved into his own apartment. He had me over to the place and stood grinning at the foot of bunk beds. "You're on top," he told me. I got my clothes, my records, and my ball glove from my mom's, and moved in with Tommy that night.

TOMMY CALLED IT GETTING back to nature. On weekends, we'd go exploring—Tommy, Jules and me. Topanga Canyon Park held endless possibilities for us to get lost in Tommy's wide-open world.

"Walk."

"What, Tommy?"

"What are you doing?"

"You know what I'm doing."

"But I want you to tell us."

"I'm not going to say it, Tommy—so stop asking."

"Do you need some help? I can send someone to help—want Jules to come help?"

Jules punched Tommy in the arm. "Shut up—I'm not going out there."

"Walk—Jules says she wants to help. Walk—you're not answering."

I pushed my way through the undergrowth and back into the clearing. I took a seat next to Jules near the fire. She sighed. "Walk, how do you put up with him?"

"Good question. I guess I'm in it for his better half."

"What half is that, friend-ol'-pal-of-mine?"

"Me—dummy," Jules said. "That's sweet, Walk."

"Who needs a beer?" Tommy asked, reaching for the Coleman.

*Pop, Pop. Pppisst*—my can exploded with foam.

"Dammit, Tommy, did you shake this?"

"Negatory, friend. Cheers!"

We clunked cans and threw them back, me leaning forward with legs spread to avoid the streaming foam.

"How far you think we hiked?"

"Not sure, but there's no going back tonight."

Tommy looked at Jules. "You okay with that?"

She smiled. "I'm okay with that. You okay with that, Walk?"

"Best," I said and rose up into a crouch poking the fire with a stick. "Gonna need more wood—I'm on it." I returned a short time later with an armload of branches and a new friend. His flashlight beam found those two huddled together. Tommy sat up for a look, his hand shielding his eyes. "Hey, take it easy on the eyeballs, Dudley Do-Right."

I dropped my load near the fire. "Guys, this is Ranger—,"

"Rick," he said, "—the name's Rick."

*Tommy let that one go, and I was glad he did.*
"He says we can't be here," I started.
Tommy broke in, "—now let him tell it, Walk. What say you, Ranger Rick?"
*And there it was.*
The ranger moved in closer—got a look at Tommy and an even better look at Jules. "Ma'am," he said tipping his hat. "This area's designated no camping." He ran his beam across the cooler, our backpacks.
Tommy stood and gave me a wink. *Here we go.* "Who says?—by who's authority?" Tommy asked the ranger.
"That's the rules. And by my authority, I guess. Sorry, but you're all going to have to leave. I can take you back down in my Jeep."
Tommy dialed the ranger in. "If this is a no camping area, where's the signs?"
"You can't expect us to post signs across 47,000 acres of wilderness."
"No—you're right. I suppose not. But it's really okay—ya see—'cus we're not camping—nope—we're just resting before we hike back. Isn't that right, Walk?"
The ranger's beam flicked to me, to Jules, and back to Tommy. "You really don't expect me to believe that you're hiking outta here tonight—in the dark? I'm not as stupid as I look."
*Did he really just say that? I cringed awaiting Tommy's reply.*
"No—how could you be?" Tommy quipped.
Before the ranger could unravel that one, Tommy said, "Ranger Rick, can I have a word with you?" The ranger followed Tommy out to the edge of the clearing. They weren't out there long. They came back together, Tommy's arm slung across the ranger's shoulders.
Ranger Rick said, "Have a good evening, folks." He touched the rim of his hat, "Ma'am," and he was gone.
Tommy returned to his spot next to Jules without a word. He belched. Satisfied with himself, he let go a long sigh.
"Well?" Jules asked. "You gonna fill us in—what did you say to him?"
"I told him you have cancer and this was your dying wish."
Jules screamed, her fists finding Tommy's shoulder as he covered up. "You did not—you did not just do that!"
I smiled to myself, gathered up a pile of kindling and dropped it on the fire. It would be another one of those nights when we'd talk until the sun came up—never once running short of things to say. It was like that for us.

IN THE YEAR of the Bicentennial, 1976, Jules turned twenty and moved out of her parents' home. I borrowed Gil's pickup and hauled the bunk beds and my stuff to my own new place just a few miles from Tommy's. I held onto the truck to take the two of them bed shopping. Jules had to try every mattress in the place—on her back, her tummy, lying on each side. She'd call out her personal rating score, "Got that, Bucko?" and expected me to keep track of it all.

Tommy approached the first mattress he encountered, pressed his knees into its side and made exaggerated thrusting motions. "This one's good by me," he announced. Jules ignored him but he got a grin out of the creepy salesman. Tommy went on nudging the creep asking, "How's Joey Heatherton—you know, in bed?" Joey was the company's sultry advertising spokesperson. Like hard up guys were supposed to think—buy the bed and get the pretty girl.

At the counter, Jules insisted she pay for half and Tommy didn't argue. When the salesman offered their options for the free GE gift with purchase—a blender, a mixer, or a toaster—we all three looked at each other and said, "TOASTER."

I WATCHED AS SHE buttered the white bread toast, the tip of her tongue parting her lips at the corner as she spread the butter—enough, but not so much that it didn't melt in all the way—just the way I liked it. Cradling the dark slice, she passed it to me. Holding it flat, I took a salty bite from one corner. Jules speared another slice from the toaster and buttered it more liberally. She passed it to Tommy who folded it in half and pressed it whole into his mouth. He swallowed. 'She makes damn good toast, doesn't she?"

"Best," I said. I turned to Jules. "Gourmet."

"No duh—I've got mad skills," she smiled. She teased two more flimsy slices from the wrapper and deposited them into the wired slots.

Tommy put his hand atop hers on the table. "Settle something for us will ya, babe? Walk here says I do something with my face when I'm drunk and I say he's full of crap."

"The squinty eyes thing," she said without hesitation.

Before Tommy could pounce, I jumped in. "That was all her. I didn't feed her a thing."

Having presented my defense, I tilted back in my chair, arms crossed, defiant.

"Bullshit!" Tommy coughed his objection. "You two are in cahoots—always whispering your little secrets." He turned to Jules. "What the hell?—squinty eyes? I'm *that* guy? And you never told me?"

"I told you," I said.

The toaster popped and Jules buttered a piece for herself. "Wanna hear about Walk's drunk face?" she said, taking a bite.

"Bring it!" Tommy said. I just grinned, intrigued.

Jules continued, "Walk's face freezes in a perpetual smile."

"Nuh-uh," I said.

"Yeah-uh," she said. "It's cute—the girls call you Double Dimples."

They had a point. I did have them—though you'd never known it during my tour of duty with the plague—acne that fucked me over all four years of high school and then disappeared seemingly the day after graduation.

"Whoa! Did my girlfriend just call my best friend cute? That decides it—one of you must go."

"Not me!"

"Yeah, you," Jules said. "—because I'm not going anywhere." She got up and wrapped her arms around Tommy from behind, nuzzling his neck.

I watched Tommy smile, having gotten what he wanted all along. I broke up their love fest by saying, "What's a guy gotta do around here to get a flaming piece of toast?"

Jules released Tommy and resumed her station at the toaster, giving me just what I wanted.

I asked her, "So—Jules, double dimples huh? Don't suppose you've got names and numbers?"

"—Speaking of dimples," Tommy interrupted. "Jules has two sweet dimples above her ass—*ass dimples!*"

Jules smacked Tommy on the backside of his head. "My bum is between you and me so shush."

"*Ferme ta bouche*, you say?" Tommy forced his buttery kiss on her.

The sweet air crept through the open window of their new apartment as our late-night conversation lingered easy among a constellation of crumbs littering the table. The three of us huddled around a toaster. Friends—*best*.

## *Chapter Five*

My life changed forever one day at the dealership—that September 1976. The change didn't announce itself—no trumpets call or gale force winds. Instead, it crept in stealth-like with the night.

I had just put a new suspension on a '66 Mercedes convertible and pulled it around front for a customer named Whittaker. I removed the plastic protecting the leather seat and the paper mat from the floorboard. I stood at the car with the door open and the engine running. Whittaker came out of the glass doors folding his receipt. He was a tall, lanky guy. He wore a tan chamois shirt un-tucked with dark jeans pulled over his boots. His hair was dark and wavy, and he wore it slicked back. His face was tanned and heavily creased—like a sea captain—you know, been around the world, seen some things. As he approached, he reached out to add his receipt to my armload of trash. "You mind tossing this for me?"

"You might want to hang onto that," I told him.

"I don't think so," he said. He swung his long legs into the car and took the wheel with his tanned hands. He looked up at me and I saw his eyes. His eyes knocked me back. I'd never seen eyes that color before. They were light gray—like mirrors. They say Paul Newman's eyes are like that—mirrors—piercing blue under the California sky.

I stared at his eyes. It was bordering rude, I know, but he stared right back, unblinking. I saw something in his eyes—something infinite—something I didn't understand at the time.

Finally, he said, "Good luck to you," and he drove away.

As I watched his 220SL pull out of the lot and onto Santa Monica Boulevard, Tommy came up next to me.

"Sweet car," he said.

"Did you see the dude's eyes?"

"Yeah. Freaky." Tommy held out a pair of sunglasses. "He left these in the lounge."

"Ray Bans?"

"No, but just as nice."

"You think he's coming back?"

"Paid with cash. He's not coming back."

"Yours or mine?" I asked.

"Let's check it out."

Atop the file cabinet behind Tommy's desk, we kept a possession arrow—you know—like in basketball. It's how we keep track of who gets the unclaimed items left in the waiting room. It might seem like stealing to you, but Tommy always said that those people are so rich they can't keep track of their things. He's right, I guess, because no one ever came back to claim anything. Once, our receptionist, Kim, called a customer about a found item and the customer turned around and called boss Steve to complain about the call. So, we use the arrow.

That day, it pointed to the W. Tommy flipped the arrow and tossed me the sunglasses. "Lucky bastard," he said.

I didn't feel bad. He got a leather jacket once. I remember another time when Tommy brought home an abandoned scarf for Jules. She absolutely loved it. But when she asked Tommy where he got it, he couldn't lie. So she wouldn't keep it. Kim ended up with it, I think. That Kim—she's a real piece of work.

Most days, Tommy and I would leave work around the same time but that day, he had some month-end reports to do—pencil pushing he called it. I was climbing on my bike in the back lot when Jimmy came out. Jimmy is the kid that washes the cars. I say kid but he's probably early twenties, like me.

"Need a lift?" I asked.

Jimmy loped over, head hanging.

"Climb on."

Jimmy said to me, "No thanks—that's okay."

Jimmy took the bus home. I don't think he wanted us to know where he lived. But I never stopped asking him if he wanted a ride. I liked Jimmy and I sure wouldn't want to ride any bus.

"New sunglasses?" he asked.

"Yeah, you like my shades. You want 'em?"

"No thanks," he said, "chicks all over me as it is."

You got to know Jimmy. He was not that way—not cocky. He was the opposite really. Jimmy was timid to the point of uncomfortable.

"Chicks my ass," I said. "Sure I can't give you a lift?"

"No. Really. I'm good, Walk."

"Alright—if you say so."

I adjusted my new shades and gave Jimmy my best Steve McQueen before I kick-started my bike and left him there to take his old bus.

AFTER DARK, I HEADED over to Tommy and Jules' place in West Alameda. Tommy was in the shower when I got there and Jules was in the kitchen. I said hello and dropped into a chair with a view of Jules at the counter. I reached behind me and grabbed Tommy's guitar from its stand—just to have something to do with my hands.

"Play me something," Jules called, popping a black olive into her mouth. I smiled because I know that she knows that I can't play a lick. She did tell me once that I could sing. But as for the guitar?—I never really tried. I'd just goof with it to pester Tommy. Jules wouldn't let it go, "Well?" she urged. So I figured, what the heck. I watched myself place uncooperative fingers on the frets to form a G chord. I began strumming and clumsily shifted to a G6. It was something that Tommy had shown me once. Tommy could play pretty good.

"'Tequila Sunrise,'" I announced.

"Really? You sure about that?" Jules said straight.

I kept on strumming and clunked through the chord progression again. "You seriously don't hear that?"

"I hear it just fine. It's just not any 'Tequila Sunrise' I know." She came over to take the guitar from me. I hung onto it and pulled her toward me. Tommy came out of their bedroom and I let go. But not before I got a smile out of her.

Tommy stood there shirtless looking like Adonis. "Where's my shirt?"

"Which one?" she asked.

"You know—*my shirt.*"

Jules brushed past him and came out of their bedroom with a long sleeve jersey T that read—*too fast to live, too young to die*—across the back. It was a line from an Eagles tune, "James Dean". I have the same shirt.

We spent that evening drinking beer, eating Jules' homemade tacos, and listening to music. On my ride home, I remember feeling lightheaded—a parade of car lights flashing bright in my eyes—so intense.

I came in the door around 1:30, drained the Coronas, and fell into my bed. I fingered the new sunglasses that I'd tossed there earlier when I'd gotten home from work. Lying there, I put them on, and an uneasy golden fog crept over me as I drifted off to sleep.

THE NEXT DAY, TOMMY and I were sitting out back of the dealership eating from a sack of burgers. The other mechanics were eating their lunches and Jimmy was there too. Jimmy sat slouched over a can of off-brand tuna—*cat food*—the guys called it. When Jimmy finished, he tucked the can opener and old bent fork into his work pants for the next day when he'd do the same thing—he'd eat the same damn thing—every single day. There was a burger left in our bag. I tossed it to Jimmy.

Tony, one of the older mechanics, was holding court as usual. The guy was a real bullshitter. He was always going off about his so-called girlfriends—"*This girl said that, and that girl did this.*" It's all crap but it's funny. All his stories were Triple X-rated and always ended with him "*blowing like Mount Vesuvius.*"

That day after Tony "blew," I jumped in with a story of my own.

"I had a dream last night," I threw in.

Tony flung out his arms to quiet the group. "Silence," he said, "young Walk here has something to share. Go on—the floor is yours." He bowed before me like a Shakespearean actor. I instantly regretted my offering but now I was stuck.

"I was in a room full of pictures—no, they were paintings." I struggled to find the right words.

"Paintings of big-breasted women," Tony moderated as if bestowed by the crowd.

"Yeah," I said, "some of them were women, I guess."

"Bitches," Tony said. "Paintings of naked bitches."

I went on. "The paintings—they were stacked all around. They were of street people or something—their faces all staring back at me and shit."

"So you were naked," Tony said. The guys all laughed.

"No! Hell no. I wasn't naked. There were just all these paintings, and gunshots, and screaming." I rushed the story along. "There was this guy waving a gun—and a door opened—and this woman was sitting on a bed—."

"—And she was naked," Tony said.

"No," I said, "she was old, and crying, and she was . . . black."

I looked at Jimmy. His eyes met mine then dropped, his brown fingers picking at the asphalt.

"Crying?" Tony said, confused.

*I realized that the whole story—sharing my dream—was a bad idea. I hadn't even gotten to the cool part where the guy shot a bullet right through the eye of a girl in one of the paintings.*

I needed a way out. I said, "So I gave it to her until I blew like Mount Vesuvius."

All the guys busted out laughing. They thought I was just giving it to Tony all along. Everyone was cracking up. Everyone but Jimmy. Jimmy just sat there real still—just looking at me.

It was as if he knew how my story was supposed to end.

ON THAT FRIDAY, OUR drummer friend Nick's band, Ventura, was playing at this dive bar called The Stable. Tommy and Jules were grabbing a bite first, so I was meeting them there. The band was about to start by the time I parked my bike. I could hear them tuning up inside. I went in through a side door and straight to the can. Joel, the band's lead guitar player, was standing at a urinal. He had his jeans open and down around his ankles—his bare ass hanging out.

"What the hell?" I said, taking the urinal next to him.

Joel looked right at me and smiled his kooky smile. "What the hell what?"

"Dropping trou just to take a piss?"

Joel threw his head back and laughed. "Freedom, my man, sweet freedom," he said. "Why the fuck are you wearing sunglasses in the men's room?—on the prowl for your lover boy?" He grabbed me by the shoulders, making kissing noises in my face. I twisted away and zipped up. A wave a nausea hit me just then—total body rolling, head spinning, bright flashes of golden light.

I went to the sink to splash cold water on my face when Pork, the bass player, pushed in the door. "You're on," he said.

"Yeah—right," I said and shut off the spigot.

"Don't jack with me," he said, jamming a wad of paper towels into my hands as he ushered me out the door. He kept right on pushing until I was up on stage where someone handed me a guitar. I looked out to the crowd for Tommy and Jules. This was clearly a joke. Then I thought, hey, just roll with it. I adjusted my shades and gripped the guitar.

Behind me, Nick counted off one-two-three-four with his sticks and the music kicked in. I figured I was unplugged—my guitar—so I stepped up and went with it. I mimed playing that guitar to a song I'd heard the band play probably a hundred times.

I truthfully have no idea how long I was on stage muddled in that golden haze. It sure felt like I was up there a long time and even stranger—that I was actually playing. Then again, there were moments when I know damn well that I was standing in the crowd watching Joel on stage. It was like being suspended between two places at once. Spellbinding. The whole thing was one fucked up night that ended with me back home totally confused and desperate for an aspirin to ease my pounding head.

I think, at the time, all I could figure is that I'd been slipped a mickey because nothing else seemed to make any sense. I hoped that Tommy could set me straight—about what went down that night. But by morning of the next day, I'd pushed the episode aside. Buried, but not forgotten.

The following Monday, I did four oil changes, a set of brakes, two inspections, and replaced a wiper motor. Tuesday was my day off. On Wednesday, I did three more oil changes, an alignment on a '72, two inspections, and an afternoon tune-up. I was running circles around Tony, Gil, and the rest of them—fueled by some manic energy. Something was happening to me. I just didn't know what.

After work, I followed Tommy home to his place where we grilled some chicken and drank some beers. Jules came home later and joined us on the balcony. That girl looked so good in her work clothes. She worked at an insurance agency and dressed the part—a silk shirt and tailored skirt.

Tommy wanted to eat on the balcony, so he and I pulled out some chairs. The table wouldn't fit so we ate off our laps. My work shirt stunk of sweat and charcoal smoke, so I tore it off and finished eating in my T-shirt, watching Jules from behind my shades as she ate and laughed. Her laugh is the best.

Later, Jules went inside while Tommy and I chilled on the balcony, lining the rail with our empties. I took off my shades as the sky blurred orange, then purple. We talked about the old days.

"—the first book I ever read cover to cover. Stayed up all night to finish the thing in a day."

"Agreed. *Catch 22* was cool. But so was *Invisible Man*."

"Yeah, remember when Mr. Biggs got all emotional handing out copies of that—Ellison's book?"

"I thought *Invisible Man* was going to be like the movie," Tommy laughed.

"Yeah—yeah—that movie—total cheese," I said. "An invisible man walking around in a trench coat and hat—that stupid bandage around his face and those huge gloves—like no one was gonna notice."

"Yeah, but the friggin' book was wacked too," he said. "All those rich sonsabitches sitting around their club watching black boys fight it out for some spare change. Bankers and doctors yelling, 'Get in there and fight—kill him, boy.'"

"What freaked me out was then the guy mixed the wrong shit into that batch of paint."

"Paint?" Tommy said. "What about when that black kid popped a boner in front of those old white dudes because of that lady?"

Jules came back out to the balcony and sat on Tommy's lap. "What are we talking about, boys?"

"*Invisible Man*," Tommy told her.

"The book—not the movie," I added.

"The book," Jules nodded, "—got it. So why did I just hear the word boner?"

Tommy said, "Yeah—I was just reminding Walk about the part where the black boys are forced to wrestle half-naked while some old white dudes yell and call them—ya know—*names.*"

"—Don't you say that word," Jules said.

Tommy put his hands up in surrender. "Hey, Ellison's word, not mine." Then mumbled for my benefit, "The kid's boner, not mine."

I said to Jules, "It just killed me when he mixed that paint wrong. Imagine white paint peeling off buildings and bridges after someone took the time to paint all that."

Tommy laughed. "What is it with you, man? You really have a fear of messing up, don't you? Afraid you're going to forget to replace the oil plug on some rich bastard's car and get canned? Relax, Walk, I won't let Steve fire you."

"Good of you, friend."

Jules took Tommy's beer from him and finished it off. "You two are just rich. Really—do you hear yourselves?—boners and spoiled paint. You missed the whole point of the book. The poor guy is handing out what he thinks are letters of recommendation from his school and the letters are instead damning him from getting any job. The world has no place for him—he's invisible—he just doesn't know it."

Tommy took the bottle back from Jules and swirled it. Peering down the neck, he said to her, "So—I'd wrestle you naked for some spare change."

Jules grabbed the bottle and turned it bottoms up over Tommy's head. I looked on from behind the dark tint of my new sunglasses. I took a swallow of beer and shook my head smiling. "All those gallons of ruined paint," I said.

I must have had too many that night because I woke in the dark on their couch all foggy and shit. It was no big deal—I'd slept over many times before. I stood and was immediately hit by a blinding headache. Standing over the toilet, I leaned on the wall to stop the room from spinning. I was curling up back on the couch when Jules came out of their bedroom. My flush must have woken her. I could see by the streetlight coming in from the high window in the bath that she was wearing just a thin t-shirt and panties.

"Coming to bed?" she called in my direction.

I mustn't have heard her right. I rubbed my eyes, said nothing. In the dark, she must've thought I was Tommy.

"Sure?" she yawned and pulled the tee over her head. She stood there topless looking right at me. *My God.*

She tilted her head at me, sighed, and turned back into the bedroom.

I sat up on the edge of the couch stretching my neck to see. I could make out the bare curve of her back in the bed. I couldn't see Tommy anywhere.

I woke up that morning not in their apartment but in my own bed, still in my clothes and wearing the sunglasses.

It was a dream—not one I'd be sharing with my best friend.

## DISTRICT OF COLUMBIA/AUGUST 1963

The group exited Santopolo's Restaurant escorted by a security detail who led them to a line of waiting cars. A suited, well-groomed man and a young woman ignored the open door and dark-suited attendant at the second car. Instead, they hurriedly entered the backseat of the third car. The security agent scrambled over to their car intending to get in the front seat. He stopped cold when the man in the back put up a hand.

"Where to, Jack?" the driver called to the backseat.

"Just drive."

The driver, a Hollywood actor, gunned the accelerator and the car sped off. The remaining motorcade filled quickly with suits and took off, tires squealing, to catch and trail the actor's car.

In the backseat, the young woman sat board straight with her hands tucked tightly between her knees. She could feel the man's thigh pressing against her own and she tried to interpret the contact. She wondered, too, about the encounters, his lean-ins and brushes, during the cocktail reception and staff dinner they had just attended. She held her eyes forward, studying the familiar eyes of the actor that flashed in the rearview mirror as the two men exchanged words.

When the man beside her shifted his weight, she glanced his way. Her heart leapt to see that he had pulled himself out of his zipper. She fixed her eyes forward and pulled her knees up and tight.

"Sharon," the man said, "do you trust me?"

"Of course, sir. Yes," she replied.

He leaned in and kissed her softly on the side of her mouth. She smelled his brandy, tasted his cigar.

"Give me your hand," he instructed, taking it. He placed it on his crotch.

She looked for the eyes in the mirror, but they were no longer there for her. "But you're the President," she whispered, her hand paralyzed.

"Yes, I am," he said. He then reached into his breast coat pocket and pulled out a pair of sunglasses. Putting them on, he said, "There. Now I want you to imagine that I'm just another boy. One who intends to have you."

He kissed her again, harder and full on the mouth. He

slipped his hand under her hair taking the nape of her neck, gently pulling her toward him.

———

## Chapter Six

It was a week and a half before I went back to Tommy and Jules' place. *Dream*—yes, but I couldn't shake the image of Jules from that night.

Tommy insisted that I follow him home—said I'd been acting all weird and shit. He said Jules missed me.

I walked in feeling jumpy and in need of a beer, but I didn't go into the kitchen because Jules was in there. I sat down in a chair. Jules came out with two Coronas. "Beer?" she offered. I said thanks and took one. Tommy flopped on the chair beside me and she handed him the other beer. She surprised me when she turned back to me. "So, where you been, Dimples?"

I dodged her question and the conversation turned to options after we eat. They suggested live music at the Rock House. I said good with me. My beer was empty, so I set it down and grabbed Tommy's guitar. I began to pick at it when Jules returned to the kitchen. The guitar—it felt different in my hands somehow.

While Jules made a salad, I could hear her half-singing, half-humming "Tequila Sunrise". Unconsciously I began playing along. After a minute or so Jules, still humming, came out with two more beers and sat one on the floor next to my empty. "Someone's been practicing," she smiled.

As soon as she said it, both Tommy and I realized that I was actually playing—the song was there. I quickly pushed the guitar to Tommy. His eyes darted from the guitar to me and he forced a laugh. "You scare me, man," he said.

I sank into my chair to let the moment pass. Truth is—I scared myself. I hadn't been practicing and had no idea how I just played like that. I pictured that freak night not so long ago on stage at The Stable and wondered—what really went down between Joel and me and his guitar?

*What the hell was happening to me?*

It rained on and off for two days. It was gray and shitty—not at all L.A. By Monday, the sky was California clear again. My last car of the day was a new Mercedes that belonged to a Mr. Baros. I watched him drive off and then put away my tools for the day.

I was climbing on my bike when Baros's car came tearing back into the lot. *What now?*

I slipped on my shades as he pulled alongside my bike. The car window came down.

"The Mondrian," he said.

"Hotel on Sunset."

"Yeah. I have a car there."

"You need us to send a tow truck?"

"No," he said, "nothing like that. I need someone to move a car for me."

My head buzzed and my sight went fuzzy. I shook it off. Said, "Move it where?"

"A house in Reseda," he said. "Interested?"

I took off my shades and rubbed my eyes. The intense brightness began to recede. "Yeah. Sure."

"See William at the valet stand." Baros handed me a piece of paper. "Here's the home address. I need it moved tonight."

"Not a problem." I took the note. Inside was tucked a fifty.

I picked up the car, a 1965 Corolla—drove hard but clean. I parked it in the street in front of the house—nothing special. I tucked the keys under the floor mat.

I hoofed it out of the neighborhood and then hitched my way back to the Mondrian for my bike.

At home, I had a bowl of Chex for dinner and went to bed early. My head hurt.

I WOKE IN BED to the smell of a candle or incense burning—musky and sweet at the same time. My eyes fluttered open into blinding streaks of golden light. I was overwhelmed by a sickening sense that I was not in my own bed—not in my room. I tried to sit up, but my body wouldn't budge. I felt weighted, numb. Panic set in.

*There!* I could move my eyes. *Wait!* No. My eyes weren't moving—the room was moving around me. I was in a room—a hotel room. It was dark and hard to see but my eyes floated across a bed to a set of floor-to-ceiling windows. As the windows drew closer, I could see it was night outside. On the street below, car lights streaked in opposing directions. I could see billboards, and the Comedy Store—its neon lit up right across the street. I knew this street. It was Sunset. I was on Sunset Boulevard—at the spot of the Mondrian.

The scent that woke me returned—stronger now. It wasn't burning. It was perfume. The view spun and before me stood a woman. She wore a hotel robe. It was open in front exposing her breasts and the dark patch between her legs. She was beautiful.

Time rippled and I was inside her. Dream sex—detached yet vivid.

After, I was at a bedside desk. A briefcase was open before me—papers spread out—business documents. A name on a letter—Baros. The correspondence was addressed to Mr. Baros, the guy from earlier at the dealership.

Among the papers was a Polaroid of a woman with what looked to be her two young daughters. Across the top was written—*We miss you already. Love, Us.* The woman in the photograph was not the woman sitting on the bed.

THE NEXT MORNING, I visited the front desk of the dealership at my break.

"Baros—is he married?"

Kim, our receptionist, looked up from her work. "The Greek Plastique?" She knew him instantly. "He doesn't wear a ring." Her pink round face let go a smile. "I could find out."

"How?"

"Watch and learn," she said. She went to a cabinet and pulled a file. She dialed the number. "Mr. Baros, please."

"No! Don't!" I went for the phone, but she waved me off.

"Yes, I see," she said into the phone. *His secretary*—she mouthed. "This is Kimberly from Plaza Motors. I was calling to schedule Mrs. Baros's car for service. Oh, I see. Mrs. Baros drives a Volvo. My mistake. Sorry to have bothered you."

Kim hung up the phone. "See how it's done? Now tell me why you wanted to know."

"I had a dream."

"About Baros's wife you didn't know existed?"

"No. Not about his wife exactly."

"What then?"

"I don't know. I can't explain it. It was more a feeling than a dream."

"Was there sex involved?" Kim gave me a wide-eyed grin. "Talk to me, Walk."

"Forget it," I said. "Hey, is Baros's home in Reseda?"

Kim didn't have to look. "You're kidding, right?"

"Right." I turned to head back to the bays.

"This isn't over," she called after me. "I want the juicy details. I want dirt."

I TOOK A LONG drive up into the canyon that night after work. I needed to clear my head. I needed to smell the eucalyptus trees.

I leaned my bike into curve after curve until there was no more to climb. I found a spot on a park boulder overlooking the great expanse of the sprawling, sparkling city below. I don't know how anyone could see such a sight and not believe in magic. The question was—did I believe?

I'd never been one to believe in much of anything. To believe in something had only ever brought me disappointment—my parents' marriage, my baseball, a high school girlfriend. All no-shows. So I preferred the black and white—just the facts.

So the facts were this. My ability to suddenly and unexplainably play guitar was real—Tommy heard it. Jules heard it. That thing with Baros and the lady at the hotel, the Mondrian, sure seemed real. I don't know how I could have possibly imagined the details of that night—the interior of the hotel room where I've never stayed, the view of Sunset boulevard from the fourth-floor windows, the sex—*well maybe*, but the briefcase and the photo of the wife and daughters—*no way*.

And then, there was that very first dream—the room full of paintings, the gunshots, the old lady crying on the bed. And the next day, that way Jimmy was looking at me—like I'd ripped out his soul or something. Real? I had to know.

## KENNEDY ESTATE/HYANNIS PORT/AUGUST 1963

The phone from the Oval Office rang at the family compound in Hyannis Port.

"—They're gone. Missing."

The matriarch listened to her son as she stood over the wicker-backed wheelchair that contained her husband, Joe Kennedy. "Oh, Jack," she said gravely, "here's your father." She handed the phone to Joe and readied a pad and pen for him, as she'd done since the stroke took her husband's voice.

Joe Kennedy put the phone to his ear and made what sound he could to trigger his son to talk. Listening, he looked out onto the wide manicured lawn where his family played their annual Thanksgiving Day football game.

Rose watched her husband's face drain as he held the phone. He handed the phone back to her. He scribbled on the pad of paper. Rose translated to her son. "He's asking if she was an intern?" She nodded her head, yes. Joe's face showed great disdain. He scribbled again.

"He wants to know if you had her place searched?"

She nodded the affirmative to Joe.

Joe scratched—tail.

"He wants you to keep a tail on her."

Rose read, "Who was driving, Jack? Peter? Peter Lawford," she relayed to Joe.

Joe mumbled sonofabitch and pointed to the word tail again.

"He wants you to put a tail on Peter, too. Yes, uh-huh. The car, Jack. He wants to know what happened to the car?" She looked at her husband, "It wasn't one of ours."

To that, Joe grunted a Goddammit that even Jack could understand.

"He's sending some men down, Jack."

Silence.

"That's right. Yes. Goodbye, Jack." Rose hung up the phone.

Jack held the phone to his ear as the line went dead. He visualized the day of his inauguration, his triumphant 'ask not' speech and the private party later that night where his father presented him with a special gift from those who put him in office. The accompanying note read—*Jack, keep your friends close and your enemies closer. Through these glasses, you will see the world not as it appears, but as it really is and know of the depths of its wealth and power.*

That night, as Jack held the note to a flame, he pondered the black magic's role in the great promise of his next four years.

## Chapter Seven

I FOLLOWED JIMMY HOME. I watched him board near work and trailed his bus, stop by lumbering stop, heading south on Alameda. When the bus stopped at 103rd, Jimmy got off. From there, he zagged another six blocks through housing projects and entered a salmon-colored apartment building on Grape.

Weathered plywood covered the front door and nearly half of the building's windows. I could swear the cinder blocks, with their graffiti and peeling paint, called out to me like a thousand voices saying—*go back, turn around*. I tucked my bike behind a dumpster and followed anyway.

Where there should have been a door handle was a hole drilled through the plywood door. I shook out my hand like I might never see it again, then poked it through and slipped inside. In the dim light, I found his last name, Cole, on the box for apartment H. I climbed the stairs and padded through the hall—ripe with the stench of neglect and fried food.

Jimmy didn't seem surprised when he opened the door and saw me there. I stepped past him without a word.

The paintings were there—from my dream—more chaotic, more colorful than I'd remembered. I stood taking them all in—the old men, the hookers and their pimps, the shopkeepers, the mothers and grandmothers, the children. Every one of them brown-eyed. Every one of them desperate for something.

I spoke first. "Steve wasn't off when he said you were an artist with the brushes," I joked.

"I can do more than clean and shine wheels."

"I see that. These are good—you're really good."

He said to me, "That story you told—you were here."

I let his question hang. I didn't know how to answer it.

Jimmy looked away. He then said, "I want you to meet someone."

In the kitchen, an old woman was bent over a pot at her feet. She was peeling potatoes. Her head tilted up and her milky eyes found mine.

"Do I know you?" she asked, and it took me aback. She was the woman from my dream, the one crying on the bed.

Jimmy spoke. "Esse, this is Walk from work."

"Walk?"

"Jeff Walker, a friend of mine from work."

It never really occurred to me that Jimmy considered me his friend. It felt good.

"Hello," I said to her, "it's nice to meet you, ma'am."

"Likewise," she said, then turned to Jimmy. "He stayin' for supper?"

Jimmy deferred to me.

"Let me guess—*tuna*?" I joked with Jimmy.

"Potato Soup," she said, spraying spittle as her mouth formed the *p*.

*Real nice.* "Best," I replied.

Grandma Esse served her potato soup on a plate with slices of buttered French bread floating on top. I wasn't so sure at first, but it was really good—messy, but good. The bread soaked up the salty soup.

She asked me, "What is it you do?"

I smiled back at her politely, "I work with Jimmy at The Plaza. I'm a mechanic there."

"That's not what I was asking," she said.

Jimmy gave me a baffled look like—don't ask me.

I asked, "What—you mean like hobbies, ma'am?"

She seized me with her eyes and said, "In your golden slumbers, boy—I'm asking what you do in your dreams."

A lump formed in my throat. "I'm not sure what—?"

"Esse, tell Walk about the store." Jimmy saved me. He went on, "—When Esse was a little girl her father ran a corner store in Opelika, Alabama. It had a tiny four-seat lunch counter. Great granddad had no formal education but served as the druggist of sorts for the black community there."

"It was mamma that mixed the tonics," Esse said. "It was she had the gift."

"At the counter, they sold ham sandwiches, fountain soda and candy—that's it! Right, grandma?" Jimmy laughed, "Some menu, huh?"

Esse showed what remained of her teeth for the first time. "Daddy let me pick out a piece of candy on days I'd keep out of trouble," she smiled, remembering.

Esse's story didn't end well though. When she was nine, a fire took their store. The family slept in the back storeroom. Her father was out on a late delivery that night. He came back to a smoldering heap—his daughter in a neighbor's arms. His wife and young son didn't make it out. "Daddy told me we'd have to make a new start. It was then he moved us out here to California."

I didn't tell Jimmy about the sunglasses that night. What would I tell him?—I didn't know myself exactly. Esse's dream question sure struck me as odd. She called dreams golden slumbers. She said her mamma had *the gift*. I wondered if maybe Esse had it too. But surely, her family's hoodoo was not in the same realm as the sunglasses.

Riding home, I'd decided to get to the bottom of this, whatever this was. I'd start at the beginning.

I WAS STANDING AT Kim's desk when she came in. "Two weeks ago—the guy with the '66. What was his name?"

"Give me a second, will ya?" She crammed her gigantic purse into a tiny desk drawer. "What's got you all worked up? More dreams?"

"The tall guy with the weird eyes."

"They were gray—I remember him." She went to the file. "Whittaker," she said pulling it, "paid with cash."

"That's the one. What do you have on him?"

"Just that—no phone or address. Not even a first name."

"Shit!"

"Now hold on—" she said scanning the work order, "—this is different. He spells Whittacker with a *ck*."

"Yeah, and—?"

"It's a clue. Maybe he's in the entertainment biz. You know sometimes they have to change up their names because someone with the same name has already registered with SAG."

"Sag?"

"The Screen Actors Guild."

Uncle Steve, our boss, came around the corner toward Kim's desk.

"Find me something," I said leaving, "—anything."

"Fine," she called taking her seat. "But you owe me an expla—good morning Mr. Steve. A fine day to sell some shiny new cars, wouldn't you say?"

"To sell shiny new *Mercedes*, Kimberly. We sell Mercedes."

"That's why you're the boss," she chirped.

Uncle Steve smiled and kept walking right on through.

Jimmy came up to me later that day asking, "You trying to find that guy?" *Kim running off at the mouth.*

"Maybe," I said, "whatta ya got?"

"He had a case in his trunk."

"A case. What kind of case?"

"Music."
"Music? Like a guitar?"
"No. An orchestra case."
"Violin?"
"No—bigger."
"Bigger? Like a bass? Or a cello?"
"Like a cello," Jimmy said.
"Well, that's something. I'll put Kim on it."
Jimmy smiled nervously. "She's already on it," he said.

I STUCK MY HEAD inside the door, called "Toaster kitchen open for business?" I stepped in—a fresh loaf of bread swinging by my side. "Hello?"

"Come on in." It was Jules, "—be out in a sec." I dropped the loaf on the table and took a seat. Jules came out of the bedroom—her hands taming her tousled hair. She gave me a little smile as she passed on her way to the fridge where she extracted the butter. She set it down on the table. "Hi-ya," she said.

"Hey," I grinned, touching my ear. She noticed—I let go.

Tommy came in scratching his head, shirtless, jeans unbuttoned. He looked my way. "When you gonna get your own?"

I cradled the toaster in my arms and patted it on top. "But this ol' gal's a classic."

"I'm not talking about the toaster."

"What then?"

"A girlfriend, numbnuts."

I pretended to give it a think. "Ya know—the bakery girl at Vonn's is kinda cute. Heavy-set, hair net, smelly apron, and all the free donuts I can eat. I'm working up the nerve to ask her out."

"Perfect," said Tommy looming over the table. "She'll give your loaf a good squeeze."

"Don't you mean my French baguette?"

"Dream on."

"Enough, boys." Jules ended it. "Toast anyone?"

"Most appreciated," I said.

"Why certainly," she curtsied.

Tommy barked, "See what I mean?—*you two*—you need to get your own, Walker."

The bread wrapper near empty, Jules swung her bare feet onto Tommy's lap. "So, when are you going to find a girl, Walk?"

I just smiled.

"What about Jan?" she said.

"Psycho," Tommy said.

"Then what about Lori—Lori's nice."

"Porker." Tommy did it again. I reached and slapped him five.

"Hey—a little help here," Jules said to him.

"I am helping. I don't want my friend here to get saddled with Petunia Pig."

I smiled. "Thanks, friend."

"Thanks, nothing—you think I wanna be looking at that?"

"It's all about you, isn't it?" Jules said.

"Pretty much—yeah. Walk needs a smokin' hot chick. Give you a little run for the mon—"

Jules jammed a dry toast into Tommy's mouth.

I got up to stretch my legs.

Jules slapped her palm on the table. "Hey, what about Becca?"

I said, "Kinda cute—red hair."

"Wed-headed thits!" Tommy added with a mouthful.

"What?" Jules asked, perturbed.

"Red-headed tits," I clarified.

She glared at Tommy. He pointed out his mouthful and said to me, "—splain it to huh."

"Well?"

"It's a theory," I told her.

Tommy forced a swallow. "—No theory. It's a thing. Redheads have upturned tits with nipples the size of saucers. Fact."

Jules turned to me. I threw up my hands, "What the man said."

Jules' eyes narrowed on Tommy. "And you know this how?"

"I'd tell you personal experience if you promise not to hold it against me. Or better yet, you hold yours against me." He went to wrap her up in his arms, but she pulled her feet down and pushed away.

"Names—," she said, "—give me names."

Tommy spouted right off, "Lorelei."

"Stevenson?"

"Yep, and Sara."

"Sara who?"

"You don't know her. Should I go on?"

"No."

"Chrissy, Jill, Emma—"

"Stop!"

"Candy, Sprinkles, Tootsie, Betty Boop—"

I cut in—"Doesn't Betty Boop have black hair?"

"Yeah? Okay then, Ginger."

I pointed to Tommy, "Yeah-yeah. *Gilligan's Island* Ginger—major redhead tits. Undeniable," I added for Jules' benefit.

Jules popped up from the table and pulled the cord on the toaster. "The kitchen is closed."

## WHITE HOUSE/DISTRICT OF COLUMBIA/NOVEMBER 1963

U.S. Attorney General Robert Kennedy had the President on a secured line.

"Things are getting bad here, Jack. They want this thing resolved."

"Is this about those goddamn sunglasses again?"

"You know it is, Jack."

"Well, just what would they have me do? The sunglasses are gone—vanished." He paused. "Look, can't they just conjure up another pair?"

"You know it's not that simple. These people—they mean business. They—"

As was his way, Jack cut off his younger brother. "Are they threatening me? Is that what this is—a threat on the President of the United States?"

Bobby Kennedy held the phone in silence.

Jack collected himself. He was reminded of the two things that got him through the recent nightmare that was the Cuban Missile Crisis: one—his brother Bobby, and two—the sunglasses. When his Generals recommended war and taunted him for being too soft on Castro, the sunglasses revealed that they, too, behind all their public bravado, were scared shitless of an escalation. This truth brought the entire planet back from the brink of destruction.

"Look," Jack told his brother, "tell them I'll meet with them. Tell them as soon as I get back from Dallas."

"Will do, Jack," Bobby said, "I'll tell them."

Jack hung up as his Press Secretary knocked twice and entered the Oval Office bringing with him news of yet another infuriating blunder at the hands of LBJ.

## Chapter Eight

Kim held up an album from her seat behind the reception desk, a big ol' grin on her face.

"The Beatles—*Abbey Road*," I said.

"He's on here," she said real smart-like.

"Who? Who's on there?"

"Your mystery man, Whittacker, that's who."

I snatched the album from her and pulled out the liner notes. "Really? Where?"

"You won't find his name in there. The orchestra musicians were un-credited."

"Huh?"

"The Beatles producer, George Martin, he did that kind of thing. He'd bring in orchestra musicians to play on the album, but they weren't always listed by name. Un-credited."

*Where does she get this shit?* "If he's not listed, how do you know?"

"I have my sources."

"Another friend-of-a-friend deal of yours, huh?"

"You might say that. Mystery Man's name is Alistair Whittacker. He was one of four cello players on the album."

"You're crazy—you know that?" I turned to get back to work. "I'm keeping this," I said.

"No. You're not."

I kept right on walking.

"It's Peter's."

"Tell your boyfriend that I'm borrowing it then." Peter was a pompous ass, CIA or something, and generally not someone to mess with. I tucked the album under my arm and kept walking.

That night, I listened to the album, all of it, start to finish, three times. I discovered things—things I needed to talk about. I called Kim to come over. *Regrettable?—maybe—but she was already part of it.*

I hardly recognized her at the door in her bulky sweatshirt and no makeup. Normally, Kim wore her eye makeup real heavy—raccoon eyes. Tommy claimed she took two Hostess Cupcakes and mashed them into her eye sockets. "Then she eats them," he'd joke.

Anyway, first thing in the door and out of her mouth comes—"Got anything to drink?"

I got us both a Bud.

"Well?" she said, knocking back the neck.

I started. "How do you think they did it—Lennon and McCartney?"

"Did what? Write songs?"

"Not just songs—hundreds of them—hit after hit. Where did all those ideas come from—all those melodies? They couldn't even read music—never trained on the piano—admitted it themselves."

Kim guzzled her beer. "And your point is—?"

"Okay. How did these two guys—men of sizable egos mind you—agree to give equal credit to every single song?"

"Uh—duh. They wrote them together."

"In the beginning, yes. Paul has said they wrote the early songs eyeball-to-eyeball. But later it was different. Later, they brought in songs on their own and the other just helped flush it out. And who decided Lennon's name would come first?"

"He was older? Crap. I don't know."

"Kim, I want to know how you knew that Whittacker with a *ck* played on this album."

Kim hesitated. "Peter's gonna kill me."

"Peter? What's Peter have to do with this?"

Kim held up a finger—*wait*, as she emptied her bottle. "Got another?"

I got up and got her another beer.

Kim slugged her second beer half down before she said, "You wanted me to find Whittacker. Well, finding people is what Peter does." She wiped her mouth with the back of her hand.

"Wait! You didn't talk to him about this—"

"—No. No way. He was out on a surveillance one night, so I went through his stuff. I figured I could see how he does it—how the government find people. But this gets weird. Whittacker's name was in one of Peter's files."

"Our Whittacker?"

"There was a picture. Same guy—only younger. Those eyes don't lie."

"What'd the file say?"

"I don't know exactly. I kinda freaked. I scanned the page and the Beatles were all over it. I saw a snip about *Abbey Road* so I read it. It said that Alistair Whittacker played on the album. That's it. I put the files away."

"Kim, listen. Did the file mention sunglasses?"

"Sunglasses? I don't know. Why?"

I wasn't ready to tell Kim or anyone about what was happening to me. "Forget it," I said.

But she wasn't going away that easy. "Your turn," she said. "You brought me here in the middle of the night for a reason. I want to hear your grand Beatles conspiracy theory. Paul is dead—blew his mind out in a car—and all that."

"Okay," I said, realizing I had to give her something. "'Hey Jude', everyone knows that Paul wrote it for John's son, Julian."

"Common knowledge," she said.

"There it is then. How does a person write something so knowing—so personal—for someone else's kid?"

"Geez. I don't know. How?"

"It's here." I pointed to the first track, "Come Together". And it's in "Golden Slumbers", right here."

"'Golden Slumbers'? The lullaby?"

"A lullaby with that kind of angst? The song's more than that. I think golden slumbers is a state of being. Paul was singing about what he and John experienced together. '*Golden slumbers fill your eyes,* and later in the medley the lyrics '*oh yeah, all right, are you going to be in my dreams tonight.*'"

"Now you've lost me."

"Kim, can you keep a secret?"

"Of course not. But go on."

"Do you believe in co-habitation?"

She grinned. "As in roommates with benefits?"

Frustrated, I went too far. "These sunglasses," I said holding them out.

"What about them?"

"You're going to think I'm crazy," I said.

"I'm with ya so far," she quipped.

"Kim—listen—I didn't know until you made the connection with Whittacker—but Kim, listen to me. I think John and Paul swapped these sunglasses to inhabit each other—through their dreams. And not just each other, other people who unknowingly inspired John and Paul's song ideas, their music—"

"Stop! Inhabited. What? Now that's just bat-shit crazy!"

"I know—believe me, Kim—I know."

"What time is it?" she asked suddenly. Before I could answer, she stood, "Peter will be home. I gotta go."

She chugged the last of her beer, gathered up Peter's album, and was out the door.

## CBS HEADQUARTERS/NEW YORK/NOVEMBER 22, 1963

Walter Cronkite sat in the CBS Newsroom drinking his coffee as he reviewed the day's stories with his lead producers.

"Light news day, gentlemen." Cronkite shuffled his notes. "Let's see. We have the first U.S. to Japan television transmission via Relay One, the C.S. Lewis obit, may he rest in peace, and a new Disneyland Park opening in Florida. What else?"

"There's that piece on that band from England."

"Oh yes, that bit that NBC scooped us on. What do they call themselves? Beetles, like the car?"

A producer spoke up. "Beatles, with an *ea*. We have our piece—better than theirs. It ran this morning and is slated again with you on the evening edition."

"Better late than never, I suppose," Cronkite retorted, "put it in."

The door opened into the small conference room where they were meeting. A young reporter stood pale and lifeless.

"What is it?" he was asked.

"We just got a call from our Dallas affiliate. The President's been shot."

## Chapter Nine

Kim TRIED TO HIDE the ugly bruise on her forehead with heavy makeup, but she wasn't fooling me.

"You okay?"

"Yeah, why?" she said, hastily stuffing her makeup into her purse. Her eyes were wet. She stood to shimmy her skirt down and smooth it before retaking her seat. *All business.*

"Did he do this to you?"

She looked right through me and didn't answer.

"Did Peter do this?"

She snapped. "I did this, okay? It's my fault."

"Your fault? How is it your fault?"

"I shouldn't have touched his album."

"He hit you over an album?"

"I mustn't have put it back in the same spot. He noticed."

"Kim, you've got to call the cops. You've got to report him."

"Call the cops? *Call the cops!* Then what? When his cop buddies show up at my door, then what?"

"That sonofabitch hit you over an album!"

"Fuck the album. Don't you get it? This isn't about that f-ing album. It's about your mystery man—Whittacker."

"What are you talking about?"

"Look, I told you it was my fault, didn't I? He noticed the album and started asking questions. I must have mentioned Whittacker and he hit me. That's all. It wasn't him. It was me. I know better than to get into his stuff."

"Did you say anything about me . . . or the sunglasses?"

"Give me a little credit."

"*Sorry.* Sorry, I just—"

"Stop already. I get it."

"I'll talk to him," I said.

"No. No, you will not. You have no idea what he's capable of—no idea what we're into. We drop it. Right here. Right now."

The phone rang and Kim picked it up.

"Good morning, Plaza Motors, this is Kimberly. How can I help you today?"

Behind the bays, Tony was holding court again, "—so I says to her, that? That's not a dog. That thing's not big enough to make a sammich."

I took a seat on the asphalt and watched the others eat their lunches. I had to talk to Peter—see what he knows. Kim would have to understand.

I BOUGHT EVERY BEATLES album—*Meet the Beatles* right through *Let It Be*. It took me more than a few record stores to find them all. I planned to write out the lyrics to every song, first album to the last. I ended up starting with *Sergeant Pepper* because the lyrics were provided with the album—for the first time actually.

John's "Strawberry Fields" caught my attention right away. He seemed to be sharing with us his experience with the sunglasses. He opens the song by saying *living is easy with eyes closed/misunderstanding all you see*. Could he have meant that without the sunglasses, that is—without the ability to see through another's eyes—you're living blind, you can't possibly know the truth about people and things? He sings *it's getting hard to be someone but it all works out/it doesn't matter much to me*. Is John losing his individuality? Could he regret being so much a collaboration of those he's inhabited? But it all worked out, didn't it—talent-wise, for John? The verse *no one I think is in my tree/I mean it must be high or low/that is you know you can't tune in but it's all right/that is I think it's not too bad*. It sounds on the surface like typical John gibberish, but is it? Someone is in his *tree*—his head. Paul maybe? But he's also in Paul's, so it's neither here nor there—*high or low*. John sings of tuning in. Is that how he and Paul refer to it? Most assume that he was referring to drugs—but it could be the sunglasses. Consider the line in the song—*always, no sometimes, I think it's me/but you know I know when it's a dream*. That sure sounded like the sunglasses to me—transport into an altered state in which you see through another's eyes, immersed in their identity, a cocktail of two beings where *nothing is real and nothing to get hung about—Strawberry Fields Forever*.

I SPENT ENDLESS NIGHTS over the next few weeks pouring through the music of the Beatles. The deeper I got, the more I came to realize that beyond the clues and musings possibly attributable to the sunglasses, the sheer magnitude of the band's catalog spoke to things unexplainable—a higher power. Musical genius and artistry through divine intervention, or was it dark magic?

I WOKE WITH A head full of doubt. It was crazy. I was crazy—*bat-shit* crazy.

I went to the sink and splashed my face. I stared at myself in the mirror. *Same me.* I didn't look like a crazy person. I slid on the sunglasses. They didn't change a thing. *Same me.* Even their dark tint didn't hide the simple mechanic living his uncomplicated existence, nor for that matter the unsure high school kid with the bad acne.

Let's face it. I didn't have one solid shred of evidence that the sunglasses once belonged to John and Paul. Whittacker is *not* the Beatles—just some guy who *may* have crossed their path. And the lyrics? Everybody and their mother have their own interpretation of what the Beatles were trying to say. There are books on it—the hidden meanings. People just bend the words to fit their own beliefs—their own causes. As for me, I think I just wanted to explain the sunglasses and what was happening to me. That, and my misplaced belief in the legend of the star-struck musician selling his soul to the devil for a God-sent talent.

I decided to give them a rest—the sunglasses and the Beatles albums. I decided I was just going to go to work each day and hang with Jules and Tommy as much as I could. Be me—just me—*Plain Jeff.*

## CBS NEWS HEADQUARTERS/NEW YORK/DECEMBER 10, 1963

Walter Cronkite paused mid-sentence to remove his heavy glasses and rub his tired eyes. In his face, and in the faces of those gathered around him, the strain of the past week's reporting on a nation in mourning was all too evident.

At last, Cronkite spoke, "What we need, gentlemen, is something to lift the cloud off our country. We need something to smile about." He drew a long breath, "Ideas?"

His staff all began speaking at once, spouting segments new and previously back-burnered. Cronkite heard something and put up a hand, effectively halting the clamor. "That's it! That story from England." He snapped his fingers searching for the name, "That band—"

"The Beatles," someone said.

"Yes, yes, of course. The Beatles. Queue that one up for us, will ya, Sam?"

The group gathered around a small desktop monitor. On the screen came the flickering image of a lively performance by four young men in matching tight suits. A song, "She Loves You", exploded from the tiny speaker.

"That might be just the thing," Cronkite said. "That hair alone is something to write home about."

To which a bald cohort commented, "What I wouldn't do for a mop-top like that!"

"Mop-top," Cronkite chuckled, "You've got something there, Joe."

The newscast that evening prompted phone calls to radio stations nationwide. America wanted to hear more from these boys from England.

The country had turned a corner.

## Chapter Ten

Tommy folded his toast and jammed it in, butter dripping down his fingers. He swallowed, smiled to himself then looked across the table at me and said in a slow southern drawl, "—'preciate the offer, ma'am, but uh, no thank you."

I coughed up a laugh, "No way—not that again."

"Not what?" Jules looked at me, then Tommy.

"Nothing," I said.

"We never told you that story?" Tommy asked. "—'preciate the offer, ma'am," he said again, laughing.

"What?" Jules said. "Catch me up."

"Ancient history," I told her, "nothing to tell."

"High school—freshman year," Tommy started, "long before he and I were—you know—us. Walk here was, shall we say, propositioned."

"Go on—" Jules grinned.

"You wanna tell it, Walk?"

"Nah. You brought it up. You tell it."

"Like I was saying—freshman year party at Rick's house."

"Rick? Rick who? Rick Kohler?"

"One in the same," Tommy said, "and let it be known that the beer and Jim Beam were flowing."

"Compliments of his mom," I added.

"Wait. Rick's mom, Katherine Kohler, the Congresswoman?"

"She was an alderman—*alderwoman*, back then," I said.

"And she was buying booze for high school freshman?"

"—All the time. And always right there with us—drinking, hanging out, telling dirty jokes, getting all touchy-feely. Right, Walk?"

"Weirdo," Jules said.

"It gets better. So on this one particular night, she's all over Walk, hanging on his arm, rubbing his shoulders. At some point, she slinks up to him and plants a big kiss."

Jules looked at me. "Tongue?"

"Swear to God it was forked."

"So, Walk, what?" Tommy said, "—she leads you back to the bedroom and starts working the button of your jeans. Unzips you."

Jules smelled smoke—*shit, shit*—she hurriedly popped the toaster. "What the flying —?"

"Flying fuck is right," Tommy said. "So, with Walk in her greedy little hands, she drops to her knees, looks up at him like a puppy and asks—may I? To which Walk—Walk infamously says 'preciate the offer, ma'am, but no thank you."

"You told her no?"

"Yeah—basically."

"Not just *no*. He told her—no *thank you*. Total screw-up."

"That sick lady should have been thrown in jail," Jules said.

"Yeah, but instead, they made her a congressman," Tommy said. "Sent her to the big house in D.C. instead of the one at San Quentin."

Sitting back in my chair, I bit into my toast. "My near miss with fame, huh?"

Jules put a hand to her forehead. "You did good—ya know—telling her no."

"Total screw-up," Tommy said.

After a minute, Jules said, "Let's bounce—take a drive."

"Where to, my queen?"

Jules looked at me, "Ideas?"

"Laurel Canyon," I said.

She smiled.

"Laurel Canyon it is," Tommy said grabbing his keys.


IT WAS THERE, WHERE we heard it would be, at the corner of Ridpath and Kirkwood, the log cabin home known as The Tavern. We stared at the place through the windows of our parked car and agreed that, by appearances, it didn't live up to its rock and roll legend. Tommy shut off the car's engine and said, "Let's go knock."

Jules replied, "Nobody's going to *go knock*."

"Come on," he said, "let's do it—I'll do it."

"I'll do it," I offered, pulling on the door handle.

"Not without me—" Tommy said, opening his door and putting boots on the ground.

"Guys!" Jules pleaded, "nobody's going up there. I know you—you'll knock and when no one answers you'll be looking for a way in."

"She has a point," I said. "History is on her side."

"History what?" Tommy asked. "What history?"

"Junior year—Hollywood Hills."

"Not following—?"

"Leggo my Eggo."

"Huh? Oh yeah. But that was different."

"Yeah. We were kids then and now we're supposed to be adults."

Tommy wasn't listening to her. "Walk," he said.

"Yeah?"

"You with me?"

"Yep. Comrades!" And before Jules could object again, Tommy and I were bee-lining it toward the house. Jules caught up with us on the porch. I saw Tommy smile to himself when he felt Jules come up behind us. He threw out his arms enthusiastically and said to his posse, "Frank Zappa's porch, people!"

He tried the door. It was locked. He banged hard three times rattling the door on its hinges. He didn't wait for an answer and went to the front picture window, cupping his eyes and squinting to see past the tangled curtains that hung inside. I took the second turn at knocking while Jules stepped back off the porch. "What do you see?" she asked Tommy.

"Sex, drugs, and rock 'n roll."

I joined him at the window, "Let me see. Oh yeah, Jules, there's a wild orgy going on in there."

"In your dreams," she said. "Party's over—let's go boys."

I wasn't ready to give up the ghost. I started around the side of the house. I looked back to see Tommy and Jules retreating to the car. When they climbed into the backseat together, I continued around the back. I stopped to have a look in each window as I went and gave the back door a pull. With nothing to report, I circled back around the front. I saw those two were still in the backseat replaying high school moves. I found a large tree on the side lot and stood for a time leaning against its base. A car drove past but seemed unbothered by Tommy's car parked there in the street. Another car approached with headlights on but also disappeared around a curve without bother. I shook off the coming chill and let my mind wander and trip upon the stories of the fabled duck pond and tunnel. I left my post to explore the property while there was still enough light. I figured I'd find the lake if I followed the slope of the lot down. I was right. It was pond-sized, overgrown at its edges with thicket, reeds, and cattails. Bullfrogs quieted then splashed into the darkness as I approached. I stood atop an embankment looking across the water. I imagined the scene described by David Crosby as seen from Joni Mitchell's neighboring window of "bare-naked groupies wading in the moonlight."

I fingered the sunglasses in my jacket pocket and thought what a trip it would've been to have them and live in Laurel Canyon during its musical heyday—where rock's L.A. sound began. To be there when Crosby, Stills, and Nash first harmonized together at Mama Cass's place; to witness firsthand Glenn Frey, J.D. Souther and Jackson Browne in the songwriting process; to party with Zappa and his house guests.

It was pitch black when I felt my way back to the car and slid behind the wheel. I heard a soft moan from the backseat as I turned the key and steered the car down from Lookout Mountain.

I couldn't have known it at the time, but my life would, soon enough, circle back to that place.

IT WAS BUSINESS AS usual at the Plaza. The '78 model year Mercedes brought Hollywood's A-list right into our showroom. Tommy quipped that we got a better celebrity turn-out than the Academy Awards that year. Uncle Steve did switch out the carpets from standard black to ruby red during that period each year—an homage to the Oscars and no doubt the dealership's bottom line due to the influx of new car inventory. Among Hollywood's elite seen walking the Plaza's red carpet that year was Katherine Hepburn, Kurt Russell, Michael Douglas, and my personal favorite—Sly Stallone. *Yo, Adrian!* When The Duke himself made an appearance, horndog Tony leered, "Look, he got himself a spinner, boys," referring to the petite oriental on Mr. Wayne's arm.

Kim had a coded announcement she'd use to alert us in the back-of-house of a showroom sighting. On the intercom she'd say, "Louie," *for Louis B. Mayer*, "pick-up on line 3." We'd drop our tools and pile up, out of sight in the hall, to get a look at the Plastiques on Parade.

I spent my days elbow deep in grease. Tony coached young Rob through his girlfriend trouble. Gil griped about his doctors and taxes. And Jimmy—he washed and shined all the livelong day stopping only at eleven sharp to eat his tuna. He and I would often pair off while we ate. We got close then, Jimmy and me. I'd even go by his place some nights to watch him paint.

"—When a white kid is born, boy or girl, don't matter, they're given a lunchbox. And from day one that lunchbox is full. Don't matter what kind of food's in there 'cus it ain't about food. It's about nourishment. The kind that tells them that they belong, that they're part of the club that runs things. The white baby is surrounded by the mother, the father, family, neighbors, teachers—you name it, society at large, that prop them up—nourishes them. And throughout their entire lives that lunchbox, see, it never runs empty.

Now a black kid—a black kid don't get the lunchbox. They count themselves lucky if they get a sack lunch in a plain brown paper bag. It's like a temporary handout, see, and at the end of the day that used-up bag is crushed and tossed out. The black kid goes to bed at night not knowing whether another sack will be there tomorrow. And again, Walk, you know I ain't talking about food. I'm talking about belonging and acceptance. A black kid is never sure, day to day, 'bout either one.

"I had a Chuck Conners *Rifleman* lunchbox."

"Yeah, you did."

"And just let it be said—for the record," I smiled, "that there soliloquy was the most words I've heard you string together since I've known you."

Jimmy grinned at me. "Yeah? Well screw you and the horse you rode in on."

I belly-laughed at that one. "Funny," I said, then, "I don't remember the name."

"What name is that?"

"The Rifleman's horse, of course."

Jimmy picked up an empty tube of paint and pelted me with it. I searched, desperate for something within arm's reach to return fire. I paused and instead motioned toward the paintings stacked all around. "You know something, Jimmy? Not every white kid has what you got. Not every white kid has your talent."

He shook his head. "Yeah—guess so. But that *Rifleman* lunchbox of yours sure sound good to me."

"I'm sorry, Jimmy."

"Sorry got nothin' to do with it. Wasn't you did this, Walk."

"Well. I'm sorry anyway—for my kind."

Jimmy and I talked on in the dark for a good twenty minutes after we'd heard Esse's bed springs squeak when she'd climbed in for the night. Jimmy stood and went to an empty easel and floor lamp centered in what was I guess you'd call their living room—minus a couch, a rug, a tv. He spun the naked bulb in its socket and the space glowed alive. He went to a stack of canvases and carefully removed the one covered in a sheet. He placed it on the easel and removed the covering. He pulled from his shirt pocket a tattered black and white photograph and secured it with a piece of masking tape to the upper corner of the canvas, being careful not to crumble any more of the photo's singed edge.

I pulled my chair up closer and watched as he twisted a tube of paint in his strong hands and squeezed a drop of ochre onto his pallet. Near the ochre, he squeezed a pearl of cobalt, calling out the colors as he went for my benefit. He reached for a brush from those resting in a jar on the floor and brushed it across his thigh to loosen the bristles. Using the tip of the brush, he dragged the warm yellow into the cool blue.

## Chapter Eleven

---

I still hadn't told a soul about the sunglasses and what I'd been experiencing—beyond unsympathetic Kim, anyway. And though I'd set aside my far-fetched Beatles theory, the sunglasses still held a strong pull of curiosity for me. It was around that time that I'd decided to explore their potential, and the dealership with its clientele was just my window of opportunity.

Near the end of a typical day in the garage, I struck up a conversation with a plastique—a big deal businessman by the name of Lally—one of the Plaza's many new-car-every-year clients. He was standing at the front counter while Kim settled his bill for a pinstriping add-on.

"Big plans for the evening, sir?"

"What's that?"

"Got something fun planned for tonight?" I asked.

Lally turned to size me up, making intentional note of my embroidered name patch. He seamless shifted into a patronizing persona. "Fun? You ask? I don't do fun. Unlike you, my day doesn't end by clocking out at four and heading to a sports bar for fun as you call it—Walk, is it?"

"Yes, sir. I mean, no, it's Jeff—Jeff Walker."

"Clever," he said, then turned back to Kim to hurry her up.

"Almost done," Kim said, "if you could just sign here for me, we'll have you on your way."

Lally signed in a doctor's scribble, took his keys from Kim, and squared his body to mine—chest puffed. I had to laugh inside at his primordial display of dominance. That might work on his office underlings to induce panic, but I casually held my cool. He peered at his own reflection in my sunglasses as he fingered his thinning hair to one side and said, "I'd say *later* but since I don't expect you'll be attending my board-prep meeting tonight I'll bid you buh-bye." Lally held his power pose for a few empty seconds and then the Big Deal walked out.

"Flipping Plastique," Kim said over my shoulder.

"Yeah, sweet guy, right?"
"Thinks his shit don't stink."
"I'll let you know," I said.
"Huh?"
"Nothin'."

I DIDN'T KNOW WHAT to expect from Lally's evening. At the least, I thought there'd be sex with his trophy wife or girlfriend. But true to form, the Big Deal plastique actually did spend the evening in a boardroom with a bunch of cronies talking numbers and crap. Not that it wasn't entertaining to watch those bozos stroke each other's egos. I can't tell you how many times I heard—*valid point, or I concur, or good catch, correction noted*. But my favorite colloquialism had to be—*at the end of the day*. *At the end of the day, we must innovate*. *At the end of the day*, a quality product is what matters most. *At the end of the day*, we made money—for our shareholders, for us. *At the end of the day*, blah, blah, blah.

I did learn something that night. In business, you must do one or all of three things—sell more, charge more, or make it for less.

A few days later, I picked up a *Wall Street Journal* left in the customer lounge. The Big Deal's company was in there—*Seiler Electronics Posts Record Second Quarter Profits*. At the end of the article, it said the company's stock surged 12% on the news.

I had an idea, but decided it was best implemented away from the Plaza—off the job.

ON TUESDAYS, MY DAY off, I started hanging with my cousin, Frank. He's the valet at Dan Tana's, a West Hollywood hot spot where businessmen notoriously took their martini lunches and stumbled out sloppy drunk at dusk. I figured I'd walk around in their heads for the evening and see if I could pick up anything of value, you know—stock tips, insider information. So I'd tag team with Frank, wishing the businessmen a pleasant evening from behind my shades and send them off behind the wheel of their insanely expensive cars. Most of them would call it a day and go straight home to their grand estates and indulgent collections. These business moguls, they all collected *something*—from ancient Chinese pottery to Salvador Dali's—from Persian rugs to rare jazz recordings. One guy's thing was Egyptian cotton shirts. The dude had not one but five of every color hanging in a closet the size of my apartment. Some of the businessmen would leave Tana's and return to the office to get a little work done or tidy up for the day. One guy would bend this secretary over her desk before heading home to the wife and kiddies. Nearly every one of them would at some point in the evening open their briefcase to read through mail and memos, or to catch up on periodicals. Whether they were truly workaholics or read to avoid getting sucked into the family dynamic, I couldn't say. Regardless, it was this common habit that provided me my opportunity. Through their eyes, I'd keep watch for words like confidential, merger, profit projections, earnings forecast.

That winter of '77, I put my $8,643 savings to work—and work it did. My stockbroker, *yeah I had one*, wanted to know where I was getting my information. So I made up a story about my cat doing his business on the stock quote pages lining the litter box. *I'm allergic to cats.*

Uncle Steve was grooming Tommy to someday take over the dealership. I think I told you that Steve didn't have any kids of his own. He and his wife, Maureen, lost a newborn son and I guess couldn't bring themselves to try again. *So sad—such a great couple.* One day, while I was reassembling a manifold, Tommy was leaning on the fender catching up. Steve came over to Tommy to say he had some figures to review with him. I overheard Steve mention C-FROGI. Tommy chuckled at the term and Steve was about to explain it when I jumped in.

"Cash Flow Return On Gross Investment," I said.

Steve stopped. "Very good," he said.

Tommy looked at me funny, so I lied. "Guess I learned a thing or two at ol' Hollywood High." *Tommy and I both knew that the chapter on personal finance barely covered how to write out a check and balance a checkbook.*

"Yeah, I guess I was out sick that day," Tommy told Steve.

When Steve left, Tommy turned to me, "What the hell?"

I told him the truth. "I picked it up in a bar," I smiled.

## JFK MEMORIAL AIRPORT/NEW YORK/FEBRUARY 1964

Descending the stairs of the Pan Am 727, four bushy-topped young men paused amidst the riotous roar to greet the throngs gathered to celebrate their arrival. Photographers, journalists, uniformed police, and assorted New York dignitaries closed ranks around them as they triumphantly first set foot on American soil.

The four were paraded around, seemingly in circles, as the crowd pressed three-deep against the arcade rail above to get an eyeful. The one called John removed his cap, acknowledging his fans, then turned to ape for his comrades.

At last, the lads were escorted to the town cars awaiting them on the tarmac. The youngest, George, was shuffled to a sequestered car where his sister waited. She had accompanied him on the trip across the pond to nurse his cold. The other three piled into the backseat of a second Cadillac, the closing door doing little to muffle the sound that rang indistinguishable as human voices.

"I should've brought you over sooner, boys," quipped John from a window seat.

"America is quite lovely, isn't it," came agreement in a Liverpool accent from the one named Paul.

"Land of opportunity," said John in his nasal tone, "home of the free, land of the brave, and all that."

"And Elvis," added Paul, "home of Elvis."

From the middle seat cushion, the one calling himself Ringo fished out what was poking him in his posterior. "Home of Elvis and free sunglasses," he proclaimed, holding forth his find.

"I'll have those." John, the ringleader, took the shades from Ringo and slid them on. "There now," he grinned, "ready for my close-up, Mr. DeMille."

"Ready to rock the music world, more like," corrected Paul.

## Chapter Twelve

Tommy scored two tickets to a Laker's game from Uncle Steve. Jules gladly passed so T and I sat in the front row seats directly behind home bench. We could literally see the steam rising off the players' heads.

*The* Jack Nicholson was in our section. So was the TV actress Courtney Bartels—cute girl, humongous eyes. She was in the same row as us, surrounded by a herd of Hollywood bucks—big collars, big cologne, big hair.

Tommy was on his game that night at the Forum. He walked right up to three chicks in the concourse and said to them—"Hot, Hotter, Hottest. Guess which is which?" Then, just like that, he walked away. We laughed all the way back to our seats thinking about those screwy girls each thinking that they were the hottest. Even funnier, the thought of them spending the rest of the night taking inventory of each other's features. *"Jenna's tits are biggest, but her eyes are too close together, and I've got the longer legs." "Mandy? Don't get me started on those ears of hers and that frizz-job she calls hair." "My tits are by far the biggest and besides, Beth's walking around on spindles for legs."* Tommy could go on and on, voicing each character. He could've done stand-up.

Between the second and third quarters, the man himself—Nicholson—looked our way and gave me that Cheshire Cat grin of his and a two-finger salute. I figured it was probably because he and I were the only two in the place wearing shades. *Yeah—I wore them.* He must of thought I was somebody, a somebody like him.

The Lakers were kicking butt. Kareem was on fire. *Lew Alcindor—my dad insisted on calling him—"not that camel-jockey name."*

On a beer run, we bumped into a giant Indiana farm boy in a Pacers jersey. "How's that working out for ya?" Tommy railed the big bruiser. Tommy was a shit-disturber extraordinaire. He mastered at flirting with disaster. And I stood ready to defend him, always.

Lew—*Kareem* had 37 points and 24 rebounds, and the Lakers won big. When the game was over, we exited—all smiles—with the Bartels entourage. She sure gave Tommy a second look. I, meanwhile, got squeezed up against one of her pretty boys who kept high-fiving me and whooping it up in my face. *Dude—enough already.*

Outside the VIP gate, we parted ways with Courtney and her boys. I looked around for Nicholson thinking—*what if?*—but he was nowhere around.

Tommy dropped me off at my place.

I BLINKED REPEATEDLY TO shatter the golden veil that gave way to streaks of intense light reflecting off the surface of the pool water. There were voices—tinny and distant, and faces—young and beautiful, coming in and out of focus. There was a party of people lounging poolside on chairs striped black and tan. There were bursts of laughter and music coming from inside the house—all glass and lit from within. Floating towards me was a bowl of candy in bright primary colors, then eyes, big eyes, a face—Courtney's face—her hand waving off the bowl of colors. The bowl in front of me now—*not candy*—pills, tabs—a hand to my mouth. Acid dropped.

Feeling warm, relaxed—crammed together on a poolside chaise. Courtney talking—to just me—she dreams of selling cookies—start a brand—her grandma's recipe—a whispered name, *Cricket*. A squealing girl streaks by in her underwear—pink bra, black bottoms—two guys giving chase. Cricket—her grandma's pet name for her. She trusts him—this guy she's talking to.

The chairs and pool are empty now. Just us. Intimate. Alone. Her head on my chest. My nose in her hair—a clean scent. INTERUPTED—some naked dude standing over us. He's wasted and he's talking loud, saying things, saying—"Have you been in? You're going in." He's grabbing her—taking her from me. It's all arms and legs. He's got her. Fuck! That fucker. They crash into the water. He's all over her. She goes under—comes up—goes under. She's struggling. GO GET HER, I yell. But he doesn't. GET HER. GET HER, YOU STUPID FUCK! But lover boy stays on the chaise—frozen. I'm him—I'm frozen.

STOP! Now I'm yelling at the guy in the water. But he can't hear me—doesn't stop. She's under and he's laughing. Fucker. He doesn't get it.

Then,

Water up to my chin—clothes clinging. Toes desperate—searching for the bottom.

Her in my arms—weightless.

Hair covering her face. I push it back. I fight the wet tangles to push it back.

Her eyes—open, so big, so empty.

I forced myself to wake up. I laid there in my bed—shaken, shaking. I ripped the sunglasses from my eyes and threw them across the room. I told myself it was just a dream—an ordinary dream.

FUNNY HOW CERTAIN THINGS can really take hold of you. That scene at the pool—Courtney Bartels limp in my arms. It haunted me.

I lost myself in my work. I went at it so fiercely I bruised some knuckles and gashed the palm of my hand. I embraced the pain. I watched the blood drip down my wrist and thought, this, this is what death looks like—bruised and bloodied. Death is not a beautiful face—not a young face—an innocent face.

I avoided the news—didn't want to hear it. It was just a dream and I wanted desperately to keep it that way. I lost it on Tony—screamed at him to turn off his radio. "Relax man, it's just some tunes." Fuck you and fuck your tunes.

Tommy came to me later in the day. He registered my bandage and my mood. "You okay, man?" I didn't answer. He stood over me at the car. "Is this about that girl?" he asked, "the one we saw—Courtney? You know she—she drowned last night. That's what they're saying."

I slammed the hood shut almost taking Tommy's fingers off. He jumped back. "What the fuck, man?" He looked at his hand—went white. "What?" he said.

"No!" I yelled.

"No, what?"

"Just NO—fucking NO. She was going to make cookies. Sell her grandma's cookies at grocery stores."

Tommy had a blank look on his face.

The other mechanics looked on, tools in hand, motionless. Tony mumbled something—couldn't help himself. "Cookies?" he griped, "—that skinny bitch never ate a cookie in her life."

*That asshole.* "ASSHOLE!" I rushed him—threw him back. His wrench went through the car window, shattering the glass.

"Shit!" Tommy rushed in and pulled me off him. I jerked loose of his arms, tripped and stumbled away. He gave me my space but watched me with a glaring scrutiny—unsure he even knew me anymore.

Tommy took me home with him. I argued—didn't want to leave my bike. He got physical with me. He had to. I stared out the car window. I didn't say a thing. I tried to calm myself, but the flashbacks would not relent. Now all the worse knowing it was not a dream.

When we got to the apartment, I hoped that Jules would be there. She had a way of calming me down. She wasn't. Tommy put me in a chair. He brought me a water, but I wouldn't take it. He sat in the chair next to me. After a while, he asked, "What's this about, Walk?"

I just stared at the floor.

"Help me out here," he said. "I'm confused. You didn't know that girl, right? Before, when you said you couldn't help her. What did you mean? Walk—?"

"It was my fault," I said. "I should've stopped him."

"Stopped who?"

"The guy—in the pool—holding her down."

"What are you saying? That somebody—some guy—drowned her?"

"Yeah. I mean—no. He was high or something. He didn't know."

Tommy went silent—unsure how to get through to me. "Walk, I took you home last night, after the game. We were both beat, remember? I said I needed to hit the sack and you agreed but said, you joked, about hanging with Nicholson. We laughed about it. Like he was your new best friend or something because he waved to you from his seat. You went home, Walk. You went to bed with a head full of celebrities and you dreamed about her."

I shook my head. "I was there. I saw it. I saw her drown—be drowned."

"You dreamt it. You mean you dreamt you saw her drown. Right?"

"I don't know."

"Look. You saw her and you dreamed about her. That's it. It's a coincidence that you dreamed of her drowning and she did. That doesn't make it your fault. And anyway, you dreamed somebody held her under. But that's not how it happened. The news didn't say anything about that."

Jules got home. Tommy followed her into their bedroom and must have filled her in. She came right over to me with a concerned face and wanted to see my hand. She held it in hers and looked me in the eyes. What she saw caused her to bite at the corner of her bottom lip. She said nothing, but kissed my bruised knuckles and turned to Tommy. He nodded and said he'd go get us some grub.

We were alone. Jules sat on the arm of my chair.

"Sad," she sighed, "—about Courtney. She was so young, and talented, and pretty. I don't know why that matters but it always seems to, doesn't it?—that she was pretty."

I shrugged.

"So tell me, Walk. Why is this hitting you so hard?"

Only because it was Jules asking did I answer. "I guess—I guess I felt like I knew her."

"We all feel that way—don't we? We saw her grow up on TV."

"It's not like that," I said. "Not for me."

"How is it then? For you?"

"I was there—with her."

"When? At the game?"

"Yes. But at the pool too." I looked at Jules for her reaction.

"Walk—," she stopped herself. "Okay," she said, putting the back of her hand to my cheek, "—okay."

We didn't talk anymore about it. We ate the Chinese Tommy brought back and talked about other things. I thought about it though. I wondered what the two of them thought of me. I thought about the sunglasses and I cursed them. I cursed that September day they came into my life.

It got late and Tommy drove me back to the dealership for my bike. He then followed me home to my place—Jules' orders.

"I'll pay for the window," I told him.

"Don't worry about it," he said. "But do me a favor—"

"Yeah—I know—Tony. I'll apologize to him."

"Walk."

"Yeah?"

"Comrades."

"Yeah. *Comrades.*"

## LENNON ESTATE/WEYBRIDGE/APRIL 1965

Paul traveled from Jane Asher's parents' home where he'd been staying to John and Cynthia's Kenwood house. John met him at the door and the two took their guitars to an upstairs room while Cynthia entertained a friend, Maureen Cleave, in the living room.

"I want you to hear something," John said. He sat and pounded out a slow-moving rhythmic melody on his guitar. Before Paul could comment, John handed him a scribbled lyric.

"Help," Paul read the title, "—for the film."

"Yeah," John said, "but it's more than that." John gave his partner a sideways look.

"—Right then," Paul said, his gaze falling to the page. He read the lyric and instinctively pulled out what John was grinning about. He read out loud John's words of a life spinning out of control—changing in so many ways and his independence vanishing in the haze. Though John was flip about it, Paul sensed that his friend was struggling with the stress of their quick rise to success and the means by which it came.

"It's about our little secret—don't ya know," John winked.

Paul nodded. "You certain you want to do that?"

"Do what? It's a bloody song."

"I know it's a song, but it's about us too, isn't it? About what we've done—the haze."

John turned suddenly agitated. "Ah, what is it you're afraid of, Paul? That they'll find us out? That it's not just us? That it's us mixed in with a little pixie dust?"

"John—" Paul started but John cut him off.

"It's just—I'm done with it, Paul—the switching places and all the rest."

"Had enough, have you? Okay," Paul said. "We'll give it a rest then, won't we."

After a silence between them, Paul said, "Play that number of yours again for me." John played and Paul listened. On his guitar, Paul picked out a counter melody to John's, urging on the pace of it.

There was no denying their magic together. Yet they would both come to rely on the pixie dust more and more for their inspiration.

## Chapter Thirteen

Tony's radio rang through the garage while we mechanics performed transplant surgery on our cold steel patients. Almost two weeks had passed since I'd jumped Tony and smashed out the car window. Tommy covered the cost—wouldn't let me pay. And, as promised, I apologized to Tony. He shook my extended hand and kept saying—we're cool, we're cool. Courtney Bartels never came up again between us. I had not forgotten or forgiven him though—for what he'd said.

The band America was playing and Tony grunted along. When the song finished, he asked nobody in particular, "Ya'll ever had a sister golden hair surprise?"

Rob was the one among us to take the bait. "If you mean a blonde, I've had plenty."

"Not just a blonde," Tony said, "the carpet has to match the drapes."

*It never occurred to me that America's song might have been about that. Leave it to Tony—the horndog.*

"Damn!" Rob followed. "Is that what that song's about? Damn."

Tony danced a jig as he grunt-sang, "…but I got so darned depressed that I fixed my sights on Sunday and got the two of us undressed. I can't live without you sister golden hair surprise, do-da-do, can't you see it in these eyes."

I had to smile. Tony's such a goofball. Tommy always said, "He's a goof, but he's our goof."

On the radio, there was a news break—something about Courtney. Tony heard it too. He moved to turn the station but head-checked me first. I motioned to leave it. He did.

Her death was now being considered a homicide.

I didn't have a television at my place—never owned one. Jules, Tommy and I huddled around their small black and white that evening. The eleven o'clock opened with a teaser of the Bartels headline but we had to sit through two other stories and a bank of commercials before they got to her. Over stock photos of Courtney through the years, the female anchor delivered in her stoic tone the now two-week old tale of Courtney's death in the pool. Live camera shots of the house followed including an image of crime scene tape around the pool area. The anchor went on to say that the LAPD had reclassified Courtney's death as a homicide and that a male suspect, a boyfriend, was being questioned. No arrests had been made. She then threw it to a street reporter outside the Beverly Hills Police Station. The on-scene reporter repeated that a male suspect was being questioned as part of an on-going homicide investigation. He added that no name or other details were being made available at this time. He then handed it back to the news desk saying he'd remain on the scene for any further updates.

We three stared numbly at the shave cream commercial that flickered from the screen. Tommy broke the silence. "Crazy," was all he said.

I felt their eyes on me, expecting me to say something—anything. After all, it was as I'd said. She'd been drowned.

I wanted to tell them. I should've told them—about that night—about the sunglasses. But I didn't.

Instead, I said, "I hope they nail the sonofabitch."

At that, Tommy gave me a look like—*you kidding me?* And in that moment, I remember feeling my whole world tilting off center.

I was about to leave their place when a NEWS FLASH graphic broke across the TV over footage unfolding live at the police station. The reporter struggled to remain centered on camera—pressed by the surging crowd. "We have a name," he said, his hand to an earpiece. "The LAPD have released the name of Peyton Hutchins—a twenty-something male and acquaintance of Courtney at the time of her death. He's not been charged as yet but it appears only a matter of time."

Another surge rocked the reporter off balance. "Can you get that?" he said to his cameraman, spinning left. The camera panned right to catch a young man being escorted in by the police. He had a jacket over his head, but the camera caught a fleeting shot of his face.

"That's him!" Tommy yelled. "That's the guy we saw at the game. Right, Walk? That's him!"

"Yeah," I said. "But they've got the wrong guy."

"TAKE A SEAT," I was told by the cop, his eyes sparking to what I'd just told him—that I had information regarding Courtney Bartels. He returned shortly to introduce Detective Neil Brandt, the lead detective in charge of the Bartels case. Brandt led me to a broom closet of a room—two chairs and a small writing table. He looked bored. He got right down to it.

"So you knew the girl?

And you were at the party?

And you saw what exactly?"

I could tell he didn't like my answers. He didn't write anything down.

"So let me get this straight. You're telling me you don't know either Courtney Bartels or Peyton Hutchins, you weren't 'technically' at the party, but you witnessed 'some guy' drowning her, and you're 'positively' sure that Hutchins didn't do it." He looked up at me. "Have I got that right?"

I nodded. And it hit me how ridiculous I must have sounded.

Detective Brandt rapped twice on the wall and the door opened. "Sergeant, can you please escort Mr. Walker out. Thank you."

Brandt didn't get up—didn't shake my hand. He just stared at the wall and tapped his fingers on his empty note pad.

Two steps out the precinct door, I remembered something—a detail from that night. "He had a scar on his stomach," I said, "—the guy that did it."

"We'll be in touch, if needed," the cop called over his shoulder as the doors shut behind him.

I WENT BY THE house. I cruised the streets of the Beverly Hills neighborhood until I recognized the house from the news reports. I wondered, staring at the home from the street, whether some day it might be featured on those infamous *Homes of the Hollywood Stars* maps. A tear-jerk moment in an otherwise giddy star-crazed tour—yours for the price of a $5 paper map. Billed as the house where TV's Courtney Bartels drowned in a pool, her young life snuffed out in its prime. *And I did nothing to stop it.*

I got off my bike on the next street over—a spot I'd calculated to be directly behind the house. Keeping to the shadows, I cut through a ridiculously lush yard lit by landscape lights. I climbed the serpentine brick wall that separated the properties. From the top, I spied the backyard pool surrounded by yellow police tape strung from rebar stakes that punctured the carpet-like lawn.

Stepping over the sagging tape, I treaded across the pool's blue slate apron to the area of the lounge chairs. I counted six—all with their black and tan striped cushions missing—trashed or collecting dust in a police evidence room. I located what I remembered to be the chair and I ran my finger along the headrest convinced that I felt something.

I looked to the house for signs of life. Satisfied in its stillness, I sunk into the cushion-less chair. I stretched my legs out and crossed them at the ankles. I let my head fall back against the straps and closed my eyes.

The flashback came to me—streaked in golden sparks like electricity—the entire incident in nothing more than a flash. My face burned hot with sweat and my knees drew up to my chest.

I got out of the chair and crouched at the water's edge. Plunging my hand in, I watched the assault ripple across the surface. Something came over me—I can't say what—but I stood and I jumped in, feet first. I felt the water pouring over my head as my heavy boots found the bottom.

Underwater, I opened my eyes and she was there. Her eyes big—no longer sad. She smiled at me. It was as if she knew I'd gladly trade my life for hers. Was that even possible? Did the sunglasses wield that kind of magic? They showed me things, but could they take those things back—turn back time?

At the bottom of the pool, I released my last breath of air through my nose and mouth. When the bubbles cleared, I was alone—Courtney was gone. My body floated to the surface—face down, arms extended. As the water lapped against my ears, I heard a voice—muffled at first—then repeated, clear this time. "Hey, you there." I lifted my head to see a man, the homeowner, coming toward the pool. Behind him, his missus was on the phone, the cord stretched taut through the open slider. I stroked to the pool's edge and leapt out—heavy, waterlogged, dripping. I made for the wall and scaled it in a single bound. I cursed as I tripped on a path light in the neighboring yard just as a dog started in. House lights flickered on as I straddled my bike. My wet boot slipped off the kick starter. It grabbed on my second attempt and I was off—only to slam sidelong into a police cruiser crossing at the end of the lane. The cop was as surprised as I was—my face plastered against his driver side window. He and I made eye contact—*hey there*. I straightened myself on my bike seat and tore off in the direction the cop had come from. His lights and siren came to life as he spun in a U-turn. I had maybe a two-block head start on him, but he closed in fast. I up-shifted and pressed on—alternating lefts and rights. I was at a disadvantage not knowing the area—each turn a potential dead-end and capture. I heard a second and maybe even a third set of sirens echoing off the homes and surrounding hills. My wrangled heart beat all the faster. I leaned in and bore down on the throttle—my bike responding with the shrill ringing of my two-stroke at its top end. I looked back as I took the next turn and the squad car was no longer there. I turned my bike in the direction I thought to be east and didn't stop until I was on familiar turf. On La Brea, I had just slowed to cruising speed to not draw attention when a cop pulled out of a strip mall ahead of me. I followed for a block then split off toward home.

Parking my bike on the side of my apartment, I noticed the mangled frame where my license plate used to be. *Shit*.

I scrambled some eggs and sat up, waiting for the flashing lights and the knock at my door.

## EMI STUDIO NO.2/LONDON/NOVEMBER 1965

The Beatles' *Rubber Soul* album was being wrapped up. The recordings were laid down over the past thirteen days and the tracks were being mixed. Ringo and George snuck off for an afternoon break at George's home in St. John's Wood, leaving John, Paul, George Martin and the engineers to the mixing.

Songs for the album were written during and immediately following the band's August tour in the states where they spent time with Bob Dylan and the Byrds in New York, Elvis Presley in Los Angeles, and countless late nights in clubs listening to live soul.

On the steps outside the studio, John and Paul were having a smoke—Woodbines.

"Well then, what do you think?"

John took a drag, "About what?"

"*Rubber Soul*."

"It's the record on your mind, is it? Well, let's see. I certainly hope the world's had enough of our silly love songs."

"We've moved on, haven't we."

"Had our share of new influences—Yes, Paul."

"American tour was timely."

'Right again, mate." John lifted the shades from his eyes. "A golden opportunity to tune in, as it were."

"Is it obvious?"

"How so?"

"For one the title—'I'm looking Through You'. And the narrative in 'Nowhere Man' and 'Norwegian Wood'. Christ, even George's song 'Think For Yourself'."

"You think he knows?"

"Don't know. Maybe."

Norman, the engineer, stuck his head out the door. "They're ready for you, boys."

## Chapter Fourteen

As the weeks blazed into winter, I dove headlong back into the music of the Beatles. I'd decided there were far too many references in their lyrics for the sunglasses to have not played some role in their lives. I spent endless nights spinning their records and writing out lyrics. The clues were there if you knew where to look. I counted over ninety times that the word *dream* appeared in their songs. I'd pin the lyrics to my wall, attempting to piece something together—something that resembled the truth. True to form, John and Paul teased and taunted.

Take "Nowhere Man" from 1965's *Rubber Soul* album. John sings *he's a real nowhere man sitting in his nowhere land making all his nowhere plans for nobody*. Sounds like John is lost in nowhere land—a dream space between what's real and what's not. *Doesn't have a point of view knows not where he's going to*. One never knows, do they, where the golden slumbers might take them. *Nowhere man please listen you don't know what you're missing, nowhere man the world is at your command*. Is John struggling to understand the absolute power of the sunglasses put at his command? What's he missing? What brand of black magic is this?

On 1966's *Revolver*, Paul opens up "Got To Get You Into My Life" with a reference to being alone, taking a ride, uncertain what he'd find there. Taking another road where he might find another mind there. Was he singing about a path—an alternate reality—seen through the perspective of another man's mind?

Same album, Paul sings about a furtive encounter in "Here, There And Everywhere". He's there, running his hands through her hair and someone is speaking yet she doesn't know he's there. Paul's a voyeur—secretly seeing through the eyes of another. I thought of myself—on that poolside chair with Courtney. And that night on Tommy's couch—with Jules standing there.

Also on *Revolver*, in the song "I'm Only Sleeping", Paul sings about sleeping in his bed while floating miles away and watching the world passing by from his window. How else could you watch the world going by without leaving your bed? The sunglasses.

Jimmy's grandma used the term golden slumbers that first night I had dinner at their place. I took a hard look at that song—part of the medley from *Abbey Road*, side two. Paul begins, *once there was a way to get back homeward*. A longing. Are Paul and John no longer able to get back to how they used to be—just two Liverpool kids with their guitars and a limited world view? Had the sunglasses changed all that—showed them things they wished they didn't know? The end of the innocence. Paul goes on, *golden slumbers fill your eyes*. The dreams, of course, come in waves of golden light. Later, on the B-side medley, Paul sings of a boy carrying that weight a long time. Is the weight guilt for lifting ideas, music from those around him? Paul then cries out in the song a question—are you going to be in my dreams tonight? And at the end he sings about the love you take. Love you take? Stealing love, life, experiences from unknowing others?

I found it interesting that these lyrics were part of the Beatles one and only medley—shreds of song parts strung together to complete the album. It was also the only song on which George and Ringo each perform a solo. *Solo*—were those two ever part of it—the sunglasses?

Back when it all started, I stood on stage at the Stable and played guitar as—*with* Joel. The sunglasses put me there. A week later, I picked up Tommy's guitar and I could play—not perfectly, but like I never could before—and without practicing. That December, I bought myself an early Christmas present—a guitar—from a secondhand music shop—one with some age on it—a history.

You can find live music every night of the week in L.A.—at the Chez, The Rock House, The Stable, even the famous Troubadour. It was at the Troubadour that I caught Tom Waits performing a set. So much to glean from that guy—a genius talent.

I ran into Waits in the hall before he went on. I introduced myself and he was good enough to shake my hand. "You mind?" he said, lifting the sunglasses from my face. His mouth gaped open as he gave them his inspection and put them on. He spun around in them, his head skyward.

"Cosmic," he said, and handed them back to me.

On stage, he shared a story or witticism before every song; things like "*I've got my own double-cross to bear*" or "*my father was a tailpipe and my mother a tree*." After a few rare songs, he said, "This next song I wrote about a car. I think most of us, at least for a time, has lived in their car. Yeah? No? Anyway, the Eagles recorded this one—you might recognize it—or depending on how this goes," he smiled, "—maybe not."

He played and sang his song, "Ol' 55". Up there—*with him*, I felt like I too was—*riding with Lady Luck*. Toward the end of his set, he said something else that stuck with me. He said, "*If you get far enough away, you'll be on your way back home.*"


FOR WEEKS, THAT'S PRETTY much how it went—my guitar lessons. I'd show up in my shades, grab a beer, and a seat up front. I'd target a player making steady eye contact and wait for the coil of nausea and veil of gold that came not every time, but most. As the golden light splintered and broke away, I'd hold their guitar in my hands—immersed in their talent. It was like going shopping for new chords, progressions, finger styles. Each night, I'd add to my repertoire. Back at my place, I'd immediately try them on for myself. Playing consciously—on my own—seemed to complete the transfer. Only then would their talent become mine. I'd usually knock off around three a.m., sleep until six-thirty, and be at work by seven.

A good boy, a proper boy. *Plain Jeff.*


ONE NIGHT OUT FOR a guitar lesson but with time to kill, I stopped in a bar in Westwood. I was ordering a beer from the bartender when he asked, "You been in?"

*Suddenly, I'm on the lounge chair with Courtney. I hear a voice saying—"You been in? You're going in. Yeah, you're definitely going in."*

I shook off the vision. "What's that?" I asked him.

"I asked if you've been in here before."

*He's there—the naked stoner. I see his scar. I raise my eyes to see his face. Show me his face.*

I looked up at the bartender. It's him. Pretty sure it's him.

"No," I swallowed, "first time."

"Well, let me know what I can get for you."

I locked eyes with him. "My beer," I said, "I ordered a Bud."

"Right," I can get that too." He reached into the well, removed the cap in one fluid motion, and set the bottle on the bar in front of me. "Two bucks, friend."

I drank my beer and watched him—*the murdering fuck*. The waitress called him Terry. He was fucking her. I could tell. He was older than her—us, mid-thirties. He had an edge to him—a self-importance.

I finished my beer and laid a twenty on the bar. In his good time, he picked it up. He came back with my change holding out both fists. My eighteen in cash clearly in his right and nothing visible in his left. "Pick one," he grinned.

I hesitated. His head spun around the bar then he turned over his left hand, opening it to reveal a blue capsule and three colored tabs of acid.

*I saw the bowl of drugs—every color in a rainbow. I saw Courtney waving it off.*

I looked him in the eyes and pointed to the cash. He laid my bills down. "Maybe next time," he said and strode off to the opposite end of the bar.

On my way out, I took the waitress by the arm. She saw my smile and raised it with a smile of her own. "Terry," I said nodding toward the bar, "—does he have a last name?"

"Ellis," she said.

IT MUST HAVE BEEN a slow crime day because Detective Brandt took my meeting. I think I amused him. I also think the detective in him knew I wasn't telling him everything.

I gave him the name—Terry Ellis.

Brandt went away for a time and returned with a file.

"He's a two-bit dealer—small potatoes. Served eighteen months, '68, and another year on probation," Brandt said. "Clean ever since looks like. No record of violence—not so much as a lover's spat. He's your killer?"

"It wasn't like that," I said. "I told you he was wasted—gone. He didn't know what he was doing."

"Look, Walker—Hutchins goes on trial in two months for the murder of Courtney Bartels. I've been told he's on suicide watch."

"I told you—Hutchins didn't do it."

"Well, the D.A. disagrees with you."

"What would it take?" I asked, "—to convince them?"

Brandt scratched his scalp through his military cut bristle. "A shred of evidence to start, maybe a credible statement from a believable eyewitness. A motive. Or better yet—how about a confession," he chuckled, "—you got one for me?"

Frustrated, I got up and moved toward the door.

"Walker," he called.

I spun back around.

Reaching into his desk drawer, he pulled out a small banged-up license plate—my plate. He handed it to me over his desk. Before he let loose of it, he said, "Do me and yourself a favor. Stay away from that house."

## OFFICE OF THE D.A./LOS ANGELES COUNTY/NOVEMBER 1977

On one side of the conference table sat the D.A.—Andrew Kline, his Assistant Prosecutor—Emily DeBasso, and LAPD Detectives—Neil Brandt and William Leary. On the other side was Alex Ramos—Public Defender, and the accused, a boy of eighteen—Francis Peyton Hutchins.

A woman offered coffee from a tray and the two detectives accepted. She then offered soft drinks to which the boy declined. His attorney said, "Pepper, please."

Kline opened the file in front of him and kicked things off by addressing the boy. "You understand the charges against you? Aggravated assault and murder in the second degree. I'm told the trespassing charge has been dropped?" He looked to his assistant. "Correct," answered DeBasso. Kline continued, "Further, you understand that you are charged as an adult and subject to the penalties accordingly." He paused, "Should you be found guilty of course." DeBasso smiled to herself.

Peyton, as he called himself, looked at his attorney who was busy swigging his Dr. Pepper. Ramos cleared his throat. "Yes, he the defendant understands the charges." He took another gulp.

"And the charged as an adult part?" Kline pressed.

"Yeah," Ramos swallowed, "that part too." He finished his soda and crushed the can.

"Another pop?" Kline offered, exchanging eye rolls with DeBasso and the cops.

"Nah, I shouldn't. Oh, what the hell. Sure."

Kline got the attention of the woman through the glass wall and pointed to the crushed can. She nodded and got up. Kline went on, "To avoid the media circus—and for that reason alone, we are prepared to offer Mr. Hutchins a plea of manslaughter with twenty years."

Ramos took his second soda from the woman and winked his thanks. Peyton wondered if Ramos was even listening. But after another long swallow Ramos said to Kline, "You're kidding?" He looked at DeBasso. "He's kidding, right? You have no evidence—none, and no—zero witness to the crime, if there even was a crime. Someone drowned—happens every day." He looked back at Kline, "All you've got—all you have are a handful of witnesses putting my boy here at the scene. I could say that about a half-dozen other young men known to have been in the company of Miss Bartels that night."

Detective Brandt thought to himself, yes, but they weren't found at the scene with their clothes soaking wet.

Kline let Ramos finish and then said to all present, "So I take that as a no to our offer?"

Ramos slurped his soda, slapped a hand on his young client's shoulder and said, "We'll take our chances with the jury, right Champ."

DeBasso closed her file. Smiled.

## Chapter Fifteen

I WAS BECOMING A different person—and not just my fat bank account and new-found talents with the guitar. The sunglasses showed me the other side of things—the light and the dark. And in the dark, I'd lost all sense of right and wrong. I was drunk with power—the power of knowing. For the first time in my life, I felt self-assured, confident, anyone's equal; equal to the plastiques, equal to the players—both guitar and otherwise, maybe even equal to Tommy. Suddenly, what was theirs could be mine. What I failed to consider is that there'd be consequences.

I TRACKED DOWN BAROS. I followed the girl—the mistress—hung outside her Reseda house. She led me to a bar on Wilshire, and to Baros. He didn't recognize me at first—out of context and all. When the girl got up to use the restroom, I went to the booth they shared in a darkened corner.

"Mr. Baros. Hey."

"Hey yourself." He returned to his drink.

I stood there.

He looked up. "Do I know you?"

I pointed to the Mercedes emblem on my jacket. He studied my face. "Oh, yes," he said smiling, "you work for Steve."

I nodded. "I moved a car for you, remember?"

His smile faded.

"Can I sit?"

"That's not a good idea. I'm with someone."

"I saw her—pretty lady. Mrs. Baros?"

His face darkened. "Look—"

The girl returned just then. She stood looking at him expectantly.

"Melissa, this is—"

"Jeff," I said, "Jeff Walker."

"He was just leaving."

"Hello, Melissa." I moved to allow her to slide back into the booth. I then sat down beside her. "I was just telling Mr. Baros about a painting," I said.

"Are you an artist?" she asked.

"Me? No. The artist is Jimmy Cole."

"I've never heard of him."

"No. You wouldn't have. He's undiscovered so to speak." I pulled a stack of Polaroids from my pocket and handed them to her.

She obliged me and looked at them. "These are good. Look Evan."

Baros took the pics and pretended to flip through them, all the while with eyes on me.

Feeling emboldened, I dropped a bomb I'd tucked away since that night at the Hotel Mondrian—a conversation they'd shared sitting across from each other in the bathtub.

"You have a gallery opening soon," I said between them.

Baros rose up. "How did you know—"

"As a matter of fact, I do," she said laying a calming hand on Baros' arm.

"Yeah. Well, I was hoping you might consider featuring some of Jimmy's work." I pointed to the Polaroids.

She laughed, "My, your friend is bold. Isn't he, Evan?" She looked to me. "Aren't we getting a little ahead of ourselves? I'd first like to meet your—"

"Jimmy Cole," I said.

"Yes. *Jimmy Cole*. And see his work in person."

"I put his address on the pics."

She turned one over. "Jordon Downs—the projects?"

Baros smirked.

"Can I get a phone number?" she asked.

"He doesn't have one."

"How about you? Do you have one?"

I stood. "Mr. Baros knows where to find me. You can keep those," I said.

I walked away—in my head the picture of her spread eagle, feet up on the edges of the tub.

WEEKS PASSED. TOWARDS THE end of a workday, Kim came back to the bays for me. "There's somebody here to see you," she said.

"Who?"

"A lady—says her name's Melissa."

I did a sweep of the garage and saw Jimmy wringing out a chamois. I followed

Kim out front.

"Jeff," Melissa smiled when she saw me. She gave me a tight hug. I took note of Kim taking note. Melissa smelled good. She wore an off-white sweater—low cut. Her tight black pants ran to her open-toe shoes that revealed her painted toenails—same color as the night in the tub.

"Come to meet Jimmy?" I asked.

"Yes. Is it a good time?"

"Good as any." I looked and saw her familiar Corolla parked out front. "We get off at four—in twenty or so. We'll meet you at your car."

"Oh? Okay," she said.

Kim jumped in. "You're welcome to wait in the customer lounge."

"Yeah—sorry. That's good," I said, realizing it could get blazing hot this time of day.

Kim pointed Melissa toward the lounge. I went back to finish up and collect Jimmy. I had told Jimmy about Melissa and her new gallery. I had played it low-key and he probably didn't expect anything to come of it. Honestly, neither did I. He agreed to let me take some pictures and now here was Melissa to punch his ticket.

Kim was standing all chummy with Melissa when I delivered Jimmy and made the introductions. Melissa went to hug Jimmy, but he stuck out his hand. When she extended her hand to shake, he'd already pulled his back. She laughed and extended her hand again and Jimmy took it. He shook hard twice, up and down. She suppressed a laugh and said, "Well—how best to do this?"

"The paintings are at my place," Jimmy said.

"And your studio is—?"

"Not a studio. It's just where I live."

"Right—in Jordan Downs. Great. Well, let's see—how should we do this?"

"I take the bus," Jimmy said.

"Or—," she said, "—or you can ride with me. Give us a chance to get to know each other."

Kim huffed a small laugh, and I could tell Jimmy wasn't sure. Riding in a car with a white lady—a pretty white lady—was everything he was taught to avoid. He looked at me.

"It'll be fine," I said. "I'll follow you guys on my bike."

YOU SHOULD HAVE SEEN Melissa at Jimmy's. I thought she might cry when she first stood among the faces and colors of Jimmy's world. She held a hand over her mouth as her body spun mindlessly clockwise taking it all in, her eyes disbelieving.

I nudged Jimmy. "I think she might like them." He gave me a tortured smile and regressed to staring down at the splattered drop cloth that doubled as Esse's living room rug. He stood—hands crammed deep into his front pockets—rocking slowing back and forth on his heels.

For a time, it seemed Melissa was so overcome that she couldn't speak. Then able to utter only, "oh my," as she addressed individual works. But soon she found her footing and began spouting artsy phrases at a mile-a-minute; phrases like, "the ragged edge of German expressionism—an unorthodox mixing of warm and cool colors—sympathetic abstraction—powerfully biographical."

*Sounded like she knew her stuff.*

She crouched before one piece of a young boy holding the hand of his older sister. She touched the edge of the painting with her finger. "Simply heartbreaking," she murmured and lingered there seemingly inside the painting. When she suddenly popped up and embraced the whole of Jimmy, she about scared him and me half to death. She stepped back and waving at the lot of them said, "All on wood panel, I suppose?"

"Yeah," Jimmy said, "you need me to paint them on canvas?"

*Did Jimmy really just offer to repaint all of these?*

"Oh goodness no," she said, "wood panel is fine—very stable actually. Some of the great masters—Bruegel, for one—painted on wood. It's just—we're going to need frames."

Jimmy wasn't sure what to say next. "I could collect some wood—fashion something," he offered.

"No—," Melissa started and retracted, "not that whatever you'd do wouldn't be great of course, but I've got something special in mind—metal frames—burnished maybe—but definitely raw and unfinished, with soldier joints visible. And thin—for sure thin—inch and a half tops—we don't want the frames distracting in any way from your work." She looked at Jimmy. "Does something like that appeal to you?"

Jimmy nodded his head, yes, but I could tell that he was still unsure whether Melissa expected him to provide the frames. I went to his side and, feeling newly flush in my bank account, offered, "I can pay for them."

Melissa took my hand. "Very sweet," she said, "but that won't be necessary. I have a benefactor in mind who will gladly advance us an amount to cover the framing."

*My guess? Baros—the lucky guy.*

Melissa said, "My goodness—I'm getting ahead of myself, aren't I? Of course, I'm talking about a show—a one man show—your show, Jimmy. Does that sound alright?"

"Sound fine, ma'am. Just fine."

Melissa looked suddenly distracted as she began formulating a long to-do list in her head. She bid Jimmy a quick goodbye and her nervous energy carried her out of the building, me on her heels. She could've stepped on a rat in the hall and not even noticed. Almost did.

OUTSIDE IN THE HARSH daylight, I saw right away that someone was hovering near Melissa's car. I rushed ahead of her.

"Hey!" I called. "Can I help you?"

He turned to us. A punk. A threat?—maybe.

"Hep me? You wanna hep me? Look like you that need hep."

He looked past me to Melissa and made a face like somebody just jammed a finger up his nostril. "What we got here? Mmm-mmm-mm." He circled us, eel eyes on Melissa. I shadowed his moves, trying to stay between the two of them. "Mmm-mmm-mm, that fine, uh huh, sho is."

Still in her own head, Melissa appeared unaffected. She moved right past him and to her car door.

"Not so fast," he hissed, "ain't no hurry now."

Melissa fished her key out of her purse, put it in the door, and turned the lock. The punk sprang quickly, putting his ass against her door so she couldn't open it. He leaned back, juvey arms crossed, legs braced. "So this you car."

I felt my jaw tense, my fists clench.

"Of course it's my car," she said deliberately. "Now kindly step aside. We're leaving."

He didn't budge. "So this the lady's car." He looked at me. "And that you bike," he said pointing.

"Yeah," I said stepping in—"so what's it going to be? Are the lady and I leaving or are we gonna have a thing here—you and me?"

"Ah—she you girlfriend, that it? You ready to fight for her."

"If that's the way you want it, yeah."

The punk cocked an eye on me and reached around his back but stopped short of pulling out whatever he had jammed into the back of his pants. "What I want, huh. What I want. Well-well, you sho got that right. 'Cus ya see, what I want is a key. We make it boyfriend's choice, how 'bout, the lady's car here or you bike."

Visualizing him with a gun, it came to me. This was the guy from my dream. The same one who shot up Jimmy's place, put the hole in a painting.

Melissa had had enough. "How old are you?" she asked him.

"Ode enough," he smiled sick—again with the nose thing.

"Good to know, big man," she said. "So you're saying you're old enough to know that trouble here is going to land your scrawny ass in jail where we both know that you most definitely will not be the big man." She looked at me. I read her and got on my bike. She turned back to the punk, "—so either we leave here right now and you go on patrolling your kingdom here as a big man or you can find out what it's like to be somebody's bitch. Now it's your choice."

The punk stretched out his neck with a wicked twist, then pulled an empty hand from behind his back. "Damn, lady. You a real bitch, ain't ya?"

"You're damn right I am," she said.

With that, Melissa got into her car—my cue to kick start my bike, and off we went. I don't think I remembered to breathe again for two blocks.

BAROS WAS THE TOP grossing agent at CAA—Creative Artists Agency. He got his law degree from out east—Dartmouth, skipped the bar, moved to L.A. and went straight into the talent business. Having made a name for himself as a brash young grinder at William Morris Agency, he was hand-picked by Michael Ovitz himself to join the other defectors in the newly formed CAA in 1975.

I learned these things from Melissa. I also learned that Evan Baros is indeed married with two young daughters, has a thing for rare, old scotch and beautiful young women. To his credit, he drew the line to never 'diddle' with CAA's female clients. That is according to Melissa, who had convinced her heart that she was more than the flavor of the month.

I had the opportunity to see Baros again several times as Melissa's gallery opening approached. Once, I delivered Jimmy to a private dinner party where Baros along with other gallery patrons were assembled. And you know, Melissa just insisted that I join them inside. Jimmy naturally kept to himself, coming out of his shell only to deliver a one-word answer when coerced. Much to Baros' consternation, I mingled freely and held my own among them. After all, my nightly runs with L.A.'s businessmen schooled me in the language of the ruling class—cool and calculated.

Truth be told, I stalked him—Baros. Knowing that his business was trading in Hollywood talent, I was curious where the golden slumbers might take me. It was a rush really—sharing dinner and drinks with Hollywood royalty. Turned out to be all director and producer types and no stars. But through Baros, I experienced L.A.'s exclusive side—from clubbing at The Palace to cocktails at The Fountain. Me—the proverbial fly-on-the-wall.

On occasion, the outings pushed into an overnight with Melissa in Bungalow 7 at the Beverly Hills Hotel or back at the Mondrian. I'd wake up in my own bed—the taste of Glenfiddich single-malt on my tongue and encounters with the dark-haired Melissa burned into my brain.

It was becoming easier to live in someone else's life than my own and my job at the garage felt inconsequential. It didn't feel foolish to me at the time—the voyeurism—my head in the clouds. It had become my reality. But I had to admit the lines were getting blurred—their lives versus mine. It was as if I was becoming them. I'd see a face, a musician, on the streets and think—I know this person. But I didn't—not really. I'd seen them in a dream. I'd catch myself before saying hello to them. I mean—right?—they didn't know me. They knew the person I'd subbed for. McCartney summed me up nicely in his song "The Fool On The Hill"—alone on that hill watching the sun going down while the eyes in my head watch the world spinning round.

### TOMMY'S APARTMENT/WEST ALAMEDA/NOVEMBER 1977

Jules heard the door to their apartment open and looked up from her book. Tommy set his keys down and went to her for a kiss.

"Late one, huh?" she said, eyes back in the book.

Tommy leaned in and took the book from her keeping the page held open. He kissed her. She noticed his hands first—his nails full of grease. Then the smell of the garage hit her. She looked up at his white shirt—smudged with grease and grime.

"What in the world?"

"Needed me in the garage today."

"Poor baby had to work for a living today, huh?"

"Guess so."

"No seriously, what gives? Got backed up, huh?"

"Walk didn't show."

"Seriously? Is he sick?"

"Don't think so."

"What do you mean? What did he say?"

"Didn't say anything. I didn't talk to him."

"Huh?"

"He didn't call in. Just didn't show."

"We're talking about our Walk?—Mr. Reliable. That's weird."

"Weird is a good word for it. This is the third time this month. He doesn't show—doesn't call. But then shows up the next day like nothing's happened."

"You shittin' me?"

"I wish I was."

"Well, that's crap—he had to have said something."

"Yeah, he said—sorry, late night."

"That's it? That's all he said?"

"Pretty much."

In that moment, Jules considered opening up to Tommy about Walk—her own observations and suspicions. Still unsure about all of it, she said instead, "Babe, something's wrong."

"—Rob's seen him out."

"What? Drinking?"

"I guess? Rob said he's seen him twice recently—and both times Walk was sitting on a stool like a zombie or something—wearing those stupid sunglasses of his."

"He does favor those shades lately. But at night?—in a

bar?"

"That's what Rob said."

"Weird."

"We've established that."

"Well, I'll get to the bottom of this. You drag his little butt over here tomorrow after work. It's time we had toast and a talk with that boy."

---

## Chapter Sixteen

---

In this city of blue and green-eyed blondes was Jules—brown hair and brown eyes. And yet, no other California girl could come close. Tommy saw it—felt it. He was ruined. He used to tell her that—"You've ruined me, girl." "You were ruined already," she'd say smiling at him with those Natalie Wood eyes and kissing him with those gypsy lips of hers. It was all well and good for Tommy—he'd been saved. Saved from the longing and heartache that comes with searching for the one. Yeah, Tommy was ruined for sure. But I was ruined too—Jules ruined me too.

"Close your eyes," she called from outside the door. "Boys, are you closing your eyes?"

"Eyes closed," Tommy called to her—looking right at me.

I put a hand over my eyes, fingers spread, smiling back at him.

"I'm coming in," she said excitedly. "Ta-Da! Boys, you can look now."

Tommy and I both turned our heads to see. Holy crap!

Jules had cut her hair. Really cut it—like short—like a boy's cut. She pushed a hand up the back of her neck, now exposed. She moved the hand to her bangs, brushing them to one side from her new part. "Well?"

I couldn't take my eyes off her. It was Jules, but different—so different. I looked at Tommy. He didn't look happy.

Jules saw Tommy's face too. "You told me you like short hair," she said to him, her voice cracking.

"No. I didn't."

"But you did."

"But I didn't. Why would I say I like something that I don't like—never liked?"

Jules stood there—raw, exposed.

"I like it," I said.

Tommy flashed me a glare. He got up and went out to the balcony.

"It's nice," I told her. "Really cute—like Mia Farrow, and uh—Twiggy. Like Twiggy, right?"

Jules summoned a smile, but her eyes remained hurt. She sighed. "He told me, Walk. We talked about that Beatles photographer one night—how he liked her hair. That girl—Astrid."

"Astrid Kirchner," I said.

"You know her too?"

I smiled a vague smile. "Well—yeah."

She held the back of her head wishing to feel the bulk that was there just an hour ago but now was lost. She dropped her hand and went out to the balcony. Tommy opened his arms and she melted into him. Her head against his chest, she looked back at me—right into me.

*Fuck.* This was bad—real bad.

DAYS LATER, I WAS headed out. I opened my apartment door to find Jules standing there.

"Can I come in?"

"Yeah, of course," I held the door open, felt the soft skin of her arm as she brushed past me. She hadn't been to my place for a long while.

She looked around—said, "Looks the same."

"It's all I need," I said.

"Is it?" she questioned, then checked her tone. "Guitar's new."

It was propped on a stand in the corner.

"Yeah, I picked that up a couple months back. It's a Martin."

"Martin? Is that a good one?" Her fingers moved across the smooth maple of the body.

"Yeah, actually. It's got a good sound."

"And you know about that now? How a good guitar sounds?"

Her question put my guard up, so I lied to cover. "Nah, not really, just repeating what the guy who sold it to me said."

She moved toward my stack of albums. Rounding the corner, she made an audible gasp when she saw my *research*—Beatles lyrics in stacks on my barbell bench and pinned all over the wall. I don't think she knew quite what to say. She looked at one close and said, "Old school."

"Huh?"

"The Beatles—old school."

"I thought I'd learn from the best," I said.

"I guess."

Jules moved toward my bedroom, paused at the door, then went in. "Still got your helmet I see."

*It sits atop my dresser collecting dust.*

"Yeah."

"Still wear it when you visit your mom?"

"Yeah—peace of mind thing—for her."

"But you don't wear it every day. You don't wear it here," she said, suggesting my deceitfulness. She then changed the subject. "What's with the jar of dimes?"

"They're old," I said, "Mercury dimes."

She picked up the jar from my dresser and rolled its contents, examining the silver through the glass.

I told her, "My dad used to say that dimes take the least amount of space for the value."

"Yeah, I guess that's right," she said.

"He used to come into my room at night—when I was little. He'd dig into his pocket and pull out his change. He and I would pick out the dimes and put them in my little airplane bank."

"Still got it?"

"The airplane? No. Long gone—like him." I came up behind her and took the jar from her. "But I saved the dimes—the Mercury dimes anyway. Look, see the wings on his helmet? My dad said that if you sleep with a Mercury dime under your pillow, you'd dream you could fly—like magic."

She set the jar down. "Did it work?"

"No. But how I tried. Dumb kid."

"You should go see him."

I didn't respond.

She smiled a far-away smile and picked up the sunglasses from my bed. She sat down on the edge holding them. She took a deep breath, then got to why she'd come.

"What's going on with you?" she asked.

"What's going on?" I looked at her, the sunglasses.

"You're different," she said.

I forced a grin. "Different how?"

*I thought she'd bring up the Courtney Bartels thing, my sudden guitar skills, Astrid—the haircut, or my missing work.*

Instead, she said, "You eat your toast like him."

"Huh?"

"You heard me. You fold it in half now and eat it whole—like Tommy."

I laughed and it hurt her. I could see it hurt her.

She knew. *Of course she knew.*

But she couldn't know—could she?—that I'd been subbing as Tommy—to be with her.

### SURREY TOWNSHIP/EAST LONDON/OCTOBER 1965

"Come on, then."

"I'm not going. You go. Me throb and I are staying in."

"Is that how it is, John?"

"That's how it is, Paul. That's exactly how it fucking is."

"Astrid will be there, ya know, and Klaus."

"Astrid and Klaus, and Tom, Dick and Harry, and a bloody aviary of young and willing birds of every persuasion—and every last one of them wanting to give me a throw, one way or another."

"Doesn't sound so bad to me," Paul smiled. "Does it now? Get dressed, John, you and your throb. Me car's outside."

John threw on shoes and a new shirt. He grabbed his sunglasses.

"You going *there* tonight?"

"What if I am? What if I fucking am, Paul?"

"Alright by me. Sure. Just be careful, you know."

"Well okay, mum, little Johnny promises to be a good boy. Let's go."

An East London flat—a gathering of London's avant-garde. Having none of it and playing the martyr, John sequestered himself to an overstuffed chair in a corner. Conversely, Paul, accustomed to the room tilting his way, held court as his bohemian friends flitted about him—charming, witty Paul.

"Get you a drink?" A brunette in beads stood over John.

"How's that?"

"A drink?" She hung a fingertip on her bottom lip. "I noticed you didn't have one."

*Observant, this one*, John thought.

"Can I sit?"

John flared his hands. *Free world*.

She sat on the arm of his chair. "Marci," she said, offering her hand.

John took it. It was tiny—birdlike. "Bob Dylan," he said.

Marci laughed her equally tiny laugh. Then, "I know the owner. We're friends. I'm a friend of the owner."

*Got that*. John smiled at her. "I'm a friend of his." He pointed out Paul.

Again, the girl, "tee-he-he."

"I know who you are," she said, leaning in and raising his sunglasses. John could smell her arm pits. On another night, that might have been a turn on.

"It's not going to happen," he said.

"What's not going to happen?"

"You and me," he said.

She stood, beads swaying confused. "You're not a nice man," she said.

*I need you to tell me that?*


Time for that drink.

John moved through the throng of hair and haze, psychedelic garb and mindless babble. In the kitchen, he opened cabinets, removed a glass from the third door and inspected it. He blew hard into it, thought better of that and gave it a rinse in the sink. He palmed sweaty cubes from a bucket, poured himself a whiskey, and stared into the shifting shapes within his glass.

Leaning against the counter, he caught his reflection, his dark glasses, in the blackened window. He lurked there eavesdropping on a couple near the fridge.

*Teddy Boy and the Norwegian*, he christened them.

The boy in his leathers and pompadour. The footwear was off. *Get ya some bloody boots, man.*

The girl was blonde, fine features, older, an accent. Her slate blue dress clung to her tall frame, nipples presenting. *Matches her eyes, the dress does*, John thought.

The boy's talking too much—asking too many questions of her. *Ah, Teddy—you daft boy.*

John registered Teddy as having a boyish pudge, not long off the teet. John has fought the same. He likes this kid, can relate.

She was not interested—the Norwegian. John urged Teddy on. Fed him lines telepathically. Teddy was not picking up what John was laying down. *Daft boy!*

The lady's had enough—she's planning her escape.

*Enough talk, Teddy. Time for doping, groping, fucking—or whatever it is you hope to do.*

She made her move. Teddy backed out of her way and into John.

"Fuck! That's my bloody foot. *Fooock!*"

"Oh. Sorry." Teddy's eyes lit up in recognition, "Really sorry." Teddy stood there, immobilized. John squared him up, placed his hands on Teddy's shoulders, and looked him right in the eyes. "Go and get her," he told him.

"Huh? Oh, right!" Teddy spun his head, wild eyes searching. John pointed to the back door.

"Oh, right. Good. Sorry then," and Teddy was gone.

Light-footed, John climbed a found stairwell, whiskey rocks jingling. In the portrait hall upstairs, he floated door to door. Checked a knob here, listened ear-to-frame there. He pushed in a third door, saw a spectacle on the bed. *Fucking exhibitionists*. He left the door open.

A flush led him to the bathroom door where two birds flew out past him and down the hall. John locked the door behind him. Their earthy scents lingered. Sex. He sat on the loo lid coddling his glass. Looking down, he counted the round black tiles among the ivory. *Holes*. Nineteen of them. He began counting again, stopped at number nine. He poked a finger at the black space, half expecting it to plunge through. He was interrupted by a brusque assault on the door. *Occupied*. Crude, urgent knocks. *Bugger off!* The knob rattled and lurched, but held. Voices, footfalls trailed off. John's left to counting holes again. Always nineteen. Each of them impenetrable, black, cold. He's tested each one. He eyed the small tub wondering if he'd fit. He climbed in. Knees up, he rested his head back against the tiled wallboard and adjusted his shades. Settling, he took comfort in the tub's cold, porcelain embrace. He rested both hands across his chest. The Death Pose. He closed his eyes—thought of his mum, Julia. He drifted off.

John awoke to a golden voice. "Excuse all the boxes. I just moved in." His eyes tracked the voice to a face. It was the blonde. In a different apartment.

*Well, hello again, Norwegian.*

She threw her wrap on the bed already laden with clothes. "Grab a seat anywhere," she said as she headed into the bath.

*You did it, Teddy ol' boy, you found her.*

*They*, Teddy and John, noticed there wasn't a chair in the place. Teddy pulled up a box near the bed and sat. The toilet flushed. They listened as she brushed, swished, spat. She emerged raking her Nordic blonde back with wet fingers. "Pretty great, isn't it?"

Teddy popped up and pretended to take it in, confirmed

there's nothing great about it, and said, "Yeah, really great. A proper apartment."

"Views aren't much, but just look at all this dark wood. I just love it."

John thought, *Bloody Black Forest, it is. And doesn't love seem a strong word, doll? It's fucking dead trees.*

"—and check out that fireplace?"

"Does it work?"

"Of course it works. Why wouldn't it?"

"Oh, right. It probably does. I just—"

"Wine?" She asked, taking out just one glass. She poured it full and helped herself to it.

*Trouble, Teddy. Trouble.*

It's clear, to John at least, that she hadn't decided yet.

Teddy moved to her. She dropped the bottle into his fumbling hands. He found the cupboard empty, grabbed a dirty juice glass from the piled sink, and poured. He gulped to catch up. She frowned.

She sat on the edge of the bed, picking at the laundry beside her and tossed it aside. Teddy missed the signal and sat back down on the box. Again, she frowned. She finished her wine, looked at him, and sighed. She knelt in front of him, took his empty glass, and set it aside. She kissed him with her tart lips and hot tongue. Teddy reciprocated with tongue but was no match for hers. She pulled away. He wanted another go at it. Teddy shifted and his weight crumbled into the box. Stuck, he began to laugh.

Unamused, she told him, "I have to work in the morning."

"Oh, right. I should go?"

"Go or stay, it's all the same to me."

Teddy shook his ass loose from the cardboard flaps. Stood up. "I guess I'll go then."

*Fuck no, you daft boy.*

She turned away from him, slipped out of her dress, and pulled on something sheer from the bed.


Wrapped in a cocoon of tangled laundry, the girl slept.

Silently, they watched her breath rise and fall in the space below her breasts. Their eyes ran the length of her white legs spread sleepily innocent.

*I'm going to have to call it, Teddy Boy. This bird has flown.*


Teddy tore the flaps from a box and piled the cardboard into the pit of the fireplace. He lit a match and held its flame to the edge of the cardboard. The flame moved across the pressed paper consuming it like a caterpillar would a leaf. He tore flaps from the remaining boxes to feed the beast. Unsatisfied, he began dumping contents, quietly, and burning boxes whole. He stood over his creation, his hand gripping the dark wood mantle. He ran his fingers along its intricate millwork. Teddy went to the kitchen and retrieved a knife. He walked to the bed.

*What's this, Teddy?*

"Fireplace works," he said to her.

She didn't stir.

At the mantle, he pried with the knife until an edge popped loose. He gripped it and leveraged a strip free, bended nails pulling through the wood and left exposed.

Still, she slept.

Teddy chucked the wood into the fire. He sat on the floor watching the wrecked mantle burn. This is good, *they* thought.

A crowd of people stood and stared as Paul led his band mate down the stairs, John's sunglasses tucked safely into Paul's waistcoat pocket.

"Paul."

"Yes, John?"

"It's good."

"What's good, John?"

"Norwegian wood."

"Okay, John. Whatever you say. Let's just get you home to Cyn."

---

# Chapter Seventeen

At the Red Door Gallery, I watched from the street as Jimmy was introduced to one filthy-rich person after another. Them in their black formal wear and Jimmy in his plain white tee and jeans. He looked so damn uncomfortable—so out of place—but then that's exactly what Melissa was going for. *Look what I've discovered. Meet the poor black kid from the projects with the insane talent. Come, buy his art. Let's celebrate your wealth together.*

Speaking of wealth, Baros was there—with his wife. He looked almost as uncomfortable as Jimmy, keeping his distance from Melissa but sharing their secret glances. It was his wife that insisted they attend. She wasn't about to miss her best girlfriend's grand opening.

Steve was there too. You know—Uncle Steve, my boss. His bride, Maureen, looked lovely as always.

The place was packed. Time and again, I'd catch a glimpse of Jimmy extending his hand and doing that double pump of his. *Now smile—nod. That's it, Jimmy.* Melissa stayed right at his side, working her own kind of magic. Uncomfortable or not, I knew that Jimmy belonged there—his art did anyway. I watched from outside for a good while before Jimmy saw me out the window and excused himself. We met in a brotherly hug halfway up the steps.

"Just look at you," I said, "your big debut."

"Yeah, it's something, huh Walk."

"Nice crowd," I said.

"Yeah, the plastiques are out in force tonight," he said.

I belly laughed. I didn't know that he was in on that joke.

"Come in," he said, "there's wine—and plates of cheese all fancy."

"Nah," I smiled, "My tux is in storage. Besides, this is your night. You ought to get back in there. Just promise me one thing."

"What's that?"

"Promise me it won't change you—you won't let it go to your head."

Jimmy laughed, "You mean like my very own seat on the mid-town bus—gold plaque and all."

"Yeah, you'll have a reserved seat on the bus and maybe even get a brand of tuna named after you—your ugly mug right there on the can."

Jimmy snorted a laugh. He looked back inside at his future and sucked in one long breath. "See ya at the Plaza, Walk."

"Not if I see you first, Jimmy Cole."

Melissa billed Jimmy's show as *Colours of the Human Condition* and she sure did a number promoting it. She used the image of a pretty, young woman waiting on a bus from one of Jimmy's paintings as the main visual accompanied by big block letters—COLE. That's right, Jimmy was introduced to L.A.'s art scene as simply COLE—in print, on bus shelters, and even on cab tops.

As you probably guessed, Jimmy's debut was a big success. I heard Melissa sold every painting in the show. Steve and Maureen bought one of a boy wearing a Mercedes emblem—a hood ornament—around his neck. They hung it front and center in the showroom of the dealership. The talk of the show was a particular piece—a painting of a teenage girl—with an actual bullet hole through her left eye. Jimmy told me the hole was put there that night—the night of my first dream—by the same punk that fucked with Melissa and me.

As my finder's fee, I negotiated with Melissa a pre-show purchase of one of Jimmy's paintings that held special meaning to me. It was the only piece in the collection that Jimmy had painted from a photograph and one that he never intended to sell. Melissa had insisted that it be part of the show, so I secretly pre-purchased it. I had the framed art delivered to—9008 Grape, Apartment H, Los Angeles, California, 90002, Attention: Esther Suggs.

Jimmy had captured the bond perfectly—between nine-year-old Esse and the little brother she'd lost in a fire.

AFTER JULES' VISIT TO my apartment, I spent less and less time with her and Tommy. It was getting too weird. I missed them though. I missed our toaster time.

I got even closer to Jimmy then. And I continued to work on Kim to open up about what she knew. As far as I knew, she'd patched things up with her precious Peter and at least wasn't boycotting me altogether. She'd talk to me, but not about Whittacker. That just made me more determined. I had to know what she thought she was protecting me from.

I MOVED THROUGH A golden fog—found a key in the bedside table—in a drawer next to a gun, a holstered pistol. I used the key to open the locked desk drawer in the next room. In the dark, my fingers roamed across the tightly packed files and stopped at a thicker one. Clumsily, I tugged on it and the support bars came loose. *Shit.* When I pulled that file, the remaining files slunk to the bottom of the drawer. *Shit.* I laid the file on the desktop and saw it was marked Gatsby. *Code for something?* I spread the file out on the desk and, checking over my shoulder, flipped on the small desk lamp. Its light illuminated several picture frames on the desk. There was one of Kim and Peter on the beach somewhere, recent. There was also a picture of a much younger Peter—he was wearing a Police uniform—graduation day. Looks like he was a Dallas cop—I hadn't known that.

Flipping through the file, I looked for anything recognizable—a word, a name. I didn't have to go far. Lennon and McCartney were all over it—just like Kim had said. Yoko. George Martin. Abbey Road Studios. And there it was—the name, Whittacker—and a picture. *Yep, same guy.* Another name—Klaus Voorman? Whittacker again—a profile. I read some. Born in England. Royal Academy of Music. London Symphony—*wow.* Studio musician—*yep.* Parents—both deceased. One brother—also deceased. Whereabouts—Berlin, Amsterdam, Morocco, the American Northwest. I unfolded a map of the United States. It was all marked up with notes inscribed over Idaho, Alaska, and Oregon with corresponding dates. Peter was tracking someone—Whittacker most likely. I flipped ahead to the last page of the file. *Shit.* Plaza Motors—Steve Scanlon, Tommy's uncle. *Shit. Shit. Shit.* I took that page and folded it up.

I reattached the drawer brackets and rushed to rehang the files trying to keep them in the right order. Lifting the last group of files, a hook got caught on the bottom of the drawer. When I jerked it free, the bottom of the drawer came with it. *A false bottom?* I pried at the corner and lifted it out. Underneath was a thick bound document. I took it out and read the cover—The Warren Report—a bootleg photocopy it looked like. *The Fuck?* The Kennedy thing? What could any of this or Peter have to do with JFK and the assassination?

I quickly put everything back in place and relocked the file drawer. I dropped the damn key and it bounced out of sight. *Shit!* I left it. I went to Kim's purse I'd seen hanging from the closet door earlier. I tucked the page about Plaza Motors into a zippered slot—figured I'd retrieve it the next day at work.

When I turned around to leave, Peter was standing there.

Kim had big arms for a girl—like an East German swimmer. The girl had some heft.

Peter never saw it coming—the right cross that laid him out.

As fist connected with Peter's jaw, I realized it was Kim doing the swinging.

My reflex—Kim's fist.

There'd be shit to pay.

Kim missed a few days of work. I was freaking out. She came back on a Friday—told Steve a story about a death in the family. Her face turned angry when I approached her desk.

"Don't even—," she said.

I looked her over—for signs of Peter's wrath. She kept her eyes down—pretending to work—ignoring me. She looked plenty pissed but okay. I turned to leave.

"How'd you do it?"

I turned around to her. "Do what?"

"Don't fuck with me, Walker." Her voice was loud, excited. She calmed herself. "He's on to you," she said. "I hope you're ready for it."

I fisted the counter, leaning in, angry. No—fuck that—I was scared. "I'm sorry," I told her.

"Too late for sorrys," she said. Then, again, "How'd you do it?—some kind of mind control? Peter thinks I was sleepwalking, but I know better. I found this in my purse," she said, holding up the folded sheet on Plaza Motors.

"Tonight," I said.

"Can't. Tomorrow—three o'clock—Hastings Park."

Hastings Park the next day.

"Hey you—Fuckface." I looked up to see Peter coming toward me in a dead trot wearing his issue tan windbreaker and polished black Fed shoes.

*Kim set me up.*

I thought to start my bike and bolt, but he'd probably pull me off the thing and wreck the both of us.

I was wearing the shades. *Did he know about them? Did Kim tell?*

I took them off as he approached and slid them into my jacket. His eyes followed my hand inside my pocket. He jammed his meat-hook inside my jacket but left the sunglasses. Then he roughly patted me down desperate for something. *He didn't know.*

"Really?" I said, "What brings you out to the park today, Secret Agent Man?" I noted the greenish bruise line along his left jaw.

"Shut up or I'll kill you, you little shit."

"Not without an order—"

He applied a pressure point hold to my neck that hurt like hell. Tightening his grip, he barked, "I said shut it." I felt myself beginning to pass out as he added, "You'd be dead already if they didn't think you know where he is. So where is he?"

*They? Who's they?*

When he realized I was in no shape to answer, he cut me loose, but not before putting a sharp elbow to my ear. *Fuck! I really do need to start wearing my helmet.*

"Where's Whittacker?" he asked again.

I rubbed my sore ear and answered, "Who's *Shit*-tacker?"

He pounded the back of his fist into that same ear.

"Ah—fuck!" It hurt, but I pushed on. "You don't even know what you're looking for, do you? They didn't tell you. It's above your pay grade."

He cocked his fist again and I covered up.

"I'm going to enjoy it," he said, "—erasing you."

"Yeah? Who else have you erased? Anyone important I should know about?"

He grabbed my neck again. "Does the name Tippit ring a bell with you?" he said through his teeth.

"No, should it?"

He let go—pushing me up against my bike. "Figures a flunky mechanic like you wouldn't know your American History."

"Nope. Can't say that I do. I spent my history class smoking dope behind the school and feeling up my skinny, tit-less girlfriend. But wait, you couldn't mean Officer Tippit of the Dallas Police allegedly killed in the line of duty by the assassin Oswald on November 22, 1963?"

At that, Peter's hand found his shoulder strap—his gun.

I looked around at the people—witnesses all around—he clocked the same.

"Better call that in, Petey-boy. I wouldn't want to see you get busted down or worse—lose your pension."

He raised his knee and I prepared to be belly-kicked. Instead, he swiveled and kicked my bike over.

"You'll talk," he said calmly—assuredly, and strolled away in those stupid black shoes of his.

## HARTFORD RESIDENCE/INGLEWOOD/OCTOBER 1977

Peter Hartford parked on the street in front of his house but didn't go inside. Instead, he walked around the corner two blocks to a sidewalk payphone.

There he fingered his swollen jaw line and sneered. He hocked deep in his throat and spit weightily into the street. He deposited a quarter into the slot and dialed a number from memory. He counted out nine rings until his call was picked up. He was asked for a code from the male voice on the other end of the line. Peter pulled a paperback from the breast pocket of his windbreaker, thumbed open the cover, and carefully punched in the number listed there.

The call was then transferred and rang only once before another man answered. Peter never spoke a word—only listened. He took no notes but instead committed the relayed information to memory. When the man on the line finished, Peter responded by saying only, "Confirmed."

Peter plucked a dime from the coin return and dropped it in the slot. He waited on the line while he was transferred a second time. He nervously drummed his fingers on the top of the phone box as he awaited the question to which he answered, "Nothing to report."

The line went dead. Peter banged the receiver back on its hook, spit at the curb, and leisurely walked the three minutes back home, time enough for him to think through his decision to withhold the recent development involving his girlfriend, a young mechanic, and most importantly, the reemergence of the illusive Whittacker.

Peter entered his front door, fixed on handling this breach himself, his own way. Inside, he scanned the premises for anything askew as was his practice, both for reasons of his profession and because Peter demanded order. Seeing the commotion of his girlfriend's make-up left out on the kitchen counter, he pulled over the trash can and swept it all away. Another cruel lesson in submission for his live-in girlfriend.

IT CAME TO ME in fleeting fits like a dream, but not like the others—not golden.

*Something wrapped around my neck—tied. A strap of some type, synched tight.*

*My eyes trailed down to socked feet perched on a chair. A tear burned hot down my cheek. My heart racing.*

*I lifted one foot—stepped off—testing the strap. It held. Up on my toes now—the strap loosened.*

*On the edge, I stepped off—and dropped. Both hands on the strap suddenly strangling—clawing for air.*

*I flailed, tipping the chair that crashed to the floor. Someone will hear—they will come.*

*Heat behind my eyes—building. Lungs burning. My body swinging, spinning slightly clockwise.*

*I'm at a birthday party. There are faces—smiling, balloons, a cake. I'm riding a bike—a fence line, houses, trees, a park whizzing by. Images coming fast. A home—a school—children playing—a blackbird alone on a wire—a life.*

*Floating now. Twitching. Then stillness. White nothingness.*

They say you never die in your dreams—you wake up first. Not sure who *they* are—because I didn't wake up.

When I learned later that Peyton Hutchins had committed suicide awaiting trial for the murder of Courtney Bartels, I knew I had to make things right.

SHE MOTIONED TOWARD THE backroom where Terry was just rounding the corner. He clearly saw me but made himself busy with shit that could clearly wait. He filled the olives and the cherries. He wiped off the back bar and even straightened the straws. Payback, I guess, for talking to his girlfriend, the waitress.

Finally, he came over. "What'll it be?"

"Give me a Bud."

"A Budweiser for the gentleman." He put the bottle down in front of me with an exaggerated flourish. "The King of Beers—three bucks." *Price gone up.*

I drank my beer and watched him. With one elbow on the bar, he doodled on a napkin. He was left-handed. I was still watching when he grabbed his pack and headed out back for a smoke. I finished my beer and followed him.

"Bum a dart?"

He looked me up and down then held out his pack. He lit me up.

Two drags in I asked, "Hernia or appendix?"

"What?"

"Your scar—hernia or appendix?"

"—the fuck is this?"

"Simple question. I saw it the night you pulled Courtney into the pool."

He flicked his butt and dropped his arms by his sides—tensed and ready to uncoil. "And who the fuck are you?"

I pulled out my shades and slid them on. "A friend of Courtney's."

"—The fuck you are," he started, then stopped. He put on a false calm, "Can't say I know a—who'd you say?"

"Courtney. You know her. You drowned her."

With that, the murdering, drug-dealing Terry—*the fuck*—got up in my face.

## RISHIKESH/FEBRUARY 1968

At the Maharishi's meditation camp in the leafy hills, Ringo moaned inside his tent from the persistent distress the hot spices of the vegetarian curries were causing his stomach.

Outside, the Maharishi lectured in his giggly, high-pitched voice to his students—among them George, John, and Paul; their respective wives and girlfriends, along with the Beach Boys' Mike Love, Donovan, the Farrow sisters, and a group of young writers, photographers, assistants and assorted trust-funders.

Between lectures, meditation, and communing with nature, the group found sparse time to play their guitars. And when strumming turned to songwriting, mostly at Paul's hand, George was quick to intercede and remind them that this time was about meditation not music.

While George was passionate in his pursuit of enlightenment through transcendental meditation, Mia Farrow's sister, Prudence, took her spiritual awakening to an even higher dimension, spending days on end alone in her tent meditating. John took particular interest in Prudence's social abstinence and goaded her to "come out and play."

Ringo and his wife, Maureen, packed it in just a week or so after arriving. Paul and his steady, Jane Asher, returned to London after week five.

As her mental and physical state faltered, talk within the encampment swirled around Prudence and the Maharishi's hold on her. John went to Maharishi one night to hear from the holy one himself the nature of his relationship with young Prudence. There, John refused Maharishi's instruction to "Remove your sunglasses, my son. I must see your eyes, and you the truth in mine."

Hearing only denial but having seen all he needed to see, John and Cynthia, George, Patti and crew set out the next morning as a frazzled Maharishi begged an explanation for their sudden departure. John refused to give his host the satisfaction, but was finally badgered to the point of saying, "If you're so fucking cosmic, you'd know."

The dear Prudence Farrow survived the ordeal and was rewarded a song from John.

## Chapter Eighteen

I'D PUNCHED PETER OUT—*as Kim*. I subbed for her and somehow willed her to action. I willed her to dig out those files and plant a right cross on Peter's jaw. Yet I couldn't get Hutchins off that chaise in time to save Courtney. I couldn't figure out the difference between the two scenarios, but I was determined to try again.

Terry Ellis and I tussled that night in the alley behind the bar. Nothing serious, just some shoving and him spewing angry words. It was enough though. The golden haze descended and the transfer registered.

That night, Terry Ellis would walk in his sleep, dig a pad and pen out of his kitchen drawer, and write a confession—*and a damn good one if I do say so myself*. He even addressed the envelope—LAPD—and affixed his own 13-cent stamp. He walked by his ruin on his way out the door the next morning—sitting there atop the basket of outgoing mail in the lobby of his apartment building.

When confronted with his own confession, by his hand, covered in his fingerprints, Terrance Joseph Ellis, confused and incredulous, rigorously fucked himself on Detective Brandt's tape machine. Too little too late for Hutchins though. Like I told you, he'd hung himself in the detention center where the DA had sent him instead of a jail cell. I read that Peyton's family filed a wrongful death lawsuit against L.A. County with the intent to start a foundation in his name.

STANDING IN THE AISLE at Tower Records, I heard someone call my name. I looked up to see Tommy coming in the door.

"Hey," I said, "where's Jules?"

"Well, hello and how are you too," he said. "Is that my shirt?"

I looked at what I was wearing—the Eagles James Dean *too fast to live too young to die* shirt. "No—it's mine."

"You sure?—because it looks like mine." He grabbed the faded red sleeve.

"No—I mean, yes, it's mine. I got the same shirt as you. Remember?"

"No," he said, "as a matter of fact, I don't."

"So where's Jules?" I asked again.

He let go of my sleeve. "A work thing."

"It's Saturday—since when does she—"

"That fuckwad Rand—called her in for some damn thing."

"Oh."

"So, Walk—the hell you been?"

"Ah—geez—lemme think—working for you. You'd know that if you'd ever come down from that white collar box of yours and visit us working stiffs toiling away in your grease factory."

Tommy laughed, "Yeah—good one, Walk." He grabbed the music book from my hand, "—the hell is this? Beatles?"

I pulled it back. "Yeah. The Beatles," I said, "it's interesting stuff."

"Oh yeah—since when?"

"I'm learning to play."

"This stuff? Really? You know if you add another s on the end, it spells beatless?"

"Don't do that," I said.

"Don't do that," he mimicked. When I didn't volley, he said, "Yeah, Jules told me she dropped by your place—that you'd bought a guitar."

"She'd be right."

"Oh yeah. And you didn't tell me? What's with all your secrets lately?"

"No secret—just wanted a guitar."

"So mysterious," he mocked. "Listen, I can teach you everything you need to know. Take me two minutes."

"I'm sure you could."

"Ah—you're better than me at something now—that it? You'll have to play for me sometime—me and Jules."

Tommy then threw his arm across my shoulder and leaned in. "Listen, you hungry?"

"I could eat."

"Let's go then." He ripped the music book from me and stuffed it back random on the shelf.

THE WAITER SAT A fourteen-inch meat lovers between us. Leaving a pile of napkins, he offered, "Two more pints?"

"Affirmative," Tommy said. He then dug right in by bending a gooey slice in half and shoveling it in—Tommy style. He swallowed. "So, guitar, huh? I took you more for a drummer. And not just because you like to beat things," he smiled, "drummers get the girls. Which might solve your other problem."

I bit into the end of my pizza. "Do you ever stop?"

"Hard to—when it's this easy."

"So, we're back in high school huh? And I'm what—your fodder?"

"Nah—just my straight man. You are straight, aren't ya?"

"Fuck!"

"Alright, alright," he said, "just jacking with ya." He folded another slice. "What do you want to talk about? Jules—that it?—that make you happy?" He shoved in his pizza and chewed, waiting for my answer.

"Do we have to do this?"

"Yes—we do. You asked about Jules. What do you want to know? That she cut her hair like a boy's? Or that she told me that you said you liked it that way?"

"Tommy—I was just trying to—"

"Nope. Tell it to someone who gives a shit." Looking off, he downed the rest of his second beer. He then turned and gave me a long, uneasy look.

I said, "Sorry, man. I didn't mean to get between you two. I'd never—"

"Never? Good to know, friend." He tossed his uneaten crust on the platter. "We done here?"

I pulled out some bills and put them on the table.

Out in the parking lot, Tommy stopped me. "I need to show you something," he said as he pulled a ring box from his pocket. He flipped open the lid for me to see.

I remember what I felt in that moment and I'm not proud of it. I felt hurt, imploded, run over. Some kind of friend, right?—to feel that way. Somehow, I managed a more appropriate response—something like, "Tommy—that's great."

"Think so?" he said.

"Yeah—I mean—you and Jules. That's great. So—when? Does she know?"

"No. I can't seem to find the right time. Not exactly been in the same place lately."

"Same place?"

Tommy stared off. "I don't know, Walk, she's been—different."

"Different how?"

"Just different—the way she acts with me—little things."

I took him by the shoulders. "Like—?"

He raised his eyes to mine. "I don't want to lose her, Walk."

I never expected to hear those words from Tommy. Ever. I told him, "You're not losing anybody. What are you talking about?"

"Something's wrong—I feel it," he said. "It's like she's not sure about me anymore. Like I'm the one who's changed. She's changed, Walk—not me—her."

"Changed?—like what? You mean like her hair?"

"Yes and no. I can get past the haircut, but I can't buy it when she says she did it for me. She did it for somebody—but that somebody wasn't me."

"You're talking crazy. Jules loves you more than anything."

"I used to think so—"

"Listen, here's what you do. Give her the ring. Give it to her and watch her face. You'll see T. You'll see how much she loves you."

"Yeah—and what if I don't—see it?" Tommy pulled away and stared off directly into the sun. "Come over tonight, Walk."

"Sure?"

"Yeah," he said, "the three of us—like before."

"Yeah? Okay. I'll pick up some bread."

"Sure," Tommy said, "sure."

*We seemed right again. But were we? Could we ever be like before—after what I'd done?*

Tommy grabbed hold of my collar as we parted. He said, unsmiling, "I'm serious about wanting my shirt back."


I WENT BACK TO the record store after leaving Tommy. From there, I walked until I found a bench in the sun where I opened the song sheet I'd bought. The song was "Two Of Us" from the *Let It Be* album recorded in 1969 as the Beatles were breaking up. I held what was likely the last song that John and Paul wrote together though reportedly, it was mostly Paul's composition. Paul said he wrote it about Linda and the weekend drives they took together in the English countryside. But I don't believe that—the chorus suggests otherwise. Paul sings—*You and I have memories longer than the road that stretches out ahead.* He hadn't known Linda long enough at that point and the tone is melancholy. The song's about Paul and John's friendship—I'm certain of it. Seemed fitting that it was the last song they released where they sang together, just the two of them, in that magical two-part harmony that started it all. As I read the lyrics, I saw the two's relationship and their shared experience with the sunglasses laid bare for all to see.

*You and me Sunday driving, not arriving, on our way back home/We're on our way home, we're on our way home, we're going home.* The two are going home— back to how it was before—before the sunglasses.

*You and me burning matches, lifting latches, on our way back home.* Another way to say illuminating the dark and opening doors into others' private lives.

*Two of us wearing raincoats, standing solo in the sun.* The raincoats represent shelter from their past indiscretions—or a means of covering up the things they'd done.

*Standing solo in the sun.* On their own once more—*solo.* In the sun—*no place to hide.* Did this mark the end of the sunglasses? It *was* the end of the Beatles.

The song felt very personal to me. I'd burned matches and lifted latches into the lives of Tommy and Jules—Kim—Baros and Melissa—and countless others. I had changed things forever and there was no going back—no going back home for me. I'd get angry at Whittacker for dropping the sunglasses into my lap with no guidance or instruction manual. What was it he'd said to me?—"Good luck to you."

## TOMMY'S APARTMENT/WEST ALAMEDA/FEBRUARY 1978

The toaster sat cold on the table between them.
    Jules spoke. "You still think he's coming?"
    Tommy jostled the ring box buried deep in his pocket. "Said he was."
    "What's gotten into him lately? He's not the same. It's like he's in his own little world."
    "How would I know. It's not like he talks to me anymore."
    "You saw him earlier. Did he say anything?"
    "Not really."
    "What'd you two talk about?"
    "I don't know. The Beatles." Tommy looked at Jules, "You."
    "What about me?"
    Tommy's eyes trailed to the floor. "Nothing—just talk."
    "You think he's got a girl?"
    "Not unless you have a twin sister you never told me about."
    "What does that mean?"
    "You know what it means. He stacks every girl he's ever met against you and of course rejects them straight away."
    "That's sweet, but you don't really believe that?"
    "Yeah—I do."
    Jules stood. "Maybe he's drinking—or worse. You said he's been missing work and Rob's seen him out."
    "I don't think that's it."
    "Well, what then? Is this Walk breaking away—out from under your shadow?"
    "My shadow?" Tommy huffed, "Walk has always been the better man—better by a billion."

Jules got up to clear the knife and butter dish from the table. "I miss him," she said.
    "Yeah, me too."

## Chapter Nineteen

I put my key in the lock to my apartment and found the door unlocked. A dread buzzed through me and landed hard in the pit of my stomach. My hand went immediately to my jacket—I had them—the sunglasses.

I pushed the door open a crack with the toe of my boot. When it swung back my way, I lowered my shoulder and charged it with everything I had expecting a chilling resistance from whoever might be lurking behind. My unchallenged force sent the doorknob through the inside drywall and cracked the door frame at the hinges.

Inside, I saw my Martin in pieces—the neck separated, shattered—its strings sprung loose and twisted. My guitar stand was lodged in the body of the guitar. I went to the lyric wall—only some stray thumbtacks remained. My notes—the marked-up Beatles lyrics—all of it—gone. I racked my brain to remember whether I'd mentioned the sunglasses in any of it. I didn't think so—a doodle maybe.

I went to my bedroom and saw my helmet stuck—slammed—into the wall above my bed. The dresser drawers were all pulled out and turned over. I dropped to my knees and searched among the scattered clothes for my dimes. The jar was gone. I pulled myself up and sat on the edge of my bed. My hand felt something wet. I brought it to my nose—piss. *Fucking Peter.*

Days later back at the Plaza, I'd skipped lunch. I just wasn't in the mood to deal with Tony's bullshit and all the rest. Instead, I worked through lunch in the solitude of the pit under a car. Tommy came to the edge and asked if I'd take a ride with him. We used to do that kind of thing a lot—escape for an hour, just us two. Tommy and I hadn't talked since I'd bailed on him and Jules the other night.

I washed up and went out front. Tommy had already grabbed the keys to one of the demos and was waiting outside. I jumped in shotgun. Tommy swung through the lot and made a left onto Santa Monica without a word. When he remained silent, waiting at a red light I said, "Hey man, sorry about the other night."

No reaction—he didn't say a word.

"Sorry," I said again, then added, "What's up?"

When the light turned, Tommy eased down the pedal and spit it out. "It's Jules."

"Jules!" I said maybe a bit too cheery, "Did you give her the ring?"

Tommy slowly shook his head and leaked the words, "She's cheating on me."

"Impossible," I said, "—there's no way. No way in hell."

"Trust me, Walk—she is."

"With who? Did she say something?"

"Doesn't need to. I know it's happening—ah, fuck—Walk, I'm gonna be sick."

Tommy jerked the wheel, forcing the car into the lot of a paint store—skidding to a stop sideways across two spots. His door flung open. He hung his head out—convulsing in dry heaves. I leapt out and rushed around to his side. I put my hand on his shoulder as he coughed and spit. He looked up at me and I crouched beside him. His eyes were red and wet. He swiped at his dripping nose with his sleeve. "Fuck!" he screamed.

"It's okay," I told him.

"No," he said and spit. "It's not. It'll kill me, Walk. Losing Jules will kill me."

"Sorry," I said. "It's just—I can't believe it—not Jules."

Tommy sat upright and said, "Why not Jules?" Then he said, "I know about Cody."

*Shit!*

I said to him, "Tommy, that was a long time ago—high school stuff."

"Yeah? Well once a cheat—"

"Don't say that. That's not Jules. I mean—who would she—?"

"—That guy from work—her boss—fucking Rand—I don't fucking know."

"No way—Jules wouldn't. Jules loves you, man."

"I used to think so—" Tommy's chest heaved as he tried to breath. "I thought a ring might fix it—but it won't. Walk, what am I supposed to do now?"

"I don't know."

Tommy stood and hung silent for a beat, then went around to the passenger side. "Take me back, Walk."

I drove back to the Plaza, my hands wet on the wheel as the whole affair sunk in—*This was on me*. Turning off the engine, I lingered with the key in hand not knowing what to say. Tommy flipped his visor down and rubbed at his eyes. "Give me a minute," he said.

I put my hand on his knee. "Promise you won't do anything."

"Yeah, Walk, okay."

"Yeah? Okay?" I said to him, "Comrades."

Tommy wanted to smile at that but couldn't. And I wanted to take back that word—our word—and all its insincerity, but it was too late. It was *all* too late.

Inside, Kim jumped me as I passed insisting, "We have to talk."

"Can't," I said.

She stepped in front of me. "Walk—it's about Peter."

"Sorry. Peter's not my problem."

"No. It is your problem," she whispered. "He's after Tommy."

"Bullshit. Why would he—"

"To get to you. That's how they work."

"So—what? I won't talk so he's gonna hurt my friend?"

"Tommy and everyone else you love—"

I cut her off as Tommy came through the door. "Later—we'll do this later," I said.

I HAD NO INTENTION of meeting Kim later and she damn well knew it. She was waiting for me at my bike. *Smart girl.* I followed her to Huddle House. The server delivered menus and waters.

Kim started right in. "Walk, I'm scared." She looked it—not her usual rough and tumble act. "He's not who he says he is."

"Peter? He's a dick. So you're telling me that he's not?"

Kim reached across the table and grabbed my arm spilling my water. "I'm serious here. Will you just listen."

I absently wiped at the spill and let my attention settle on her.

"Thank you," she said and began to cry. She spoke between sobs, "I'm so pathetic—so fucking desperate for a boyfriend. I clung on seven fucking years. Seven years because I was afraid that without him, I'd have to face what I really am—a fat, pathetic girl—undeserving of love—meant to be alone—fucking miserable and alone."

"Don't," I said, "that's not who you are."

"Oh yeah? Look around—look around this fucking place—fucking Los Angeles. Fucking L.A. where every girl is prettier than the next—every face the benefactor of perfect genes from perfect parents who came out here for that reason—to choose among perfection—to live it—to breed it."

"They're plastiques, Kim, you know that. Pretenders—no better than you and me. What they are is not even real."

"What is real then? Answer me that. What about Peter and his secret boys club—are they real? Because what I found makes it all bullshit—what they teach us in school, the wars, our government, *fuck*—society itself. It's all crap—run by puppet masters—all of it."

Our waiter came to take our order. I told him not now. It came out forcefully and he scurried back behind his counter. I tried to get Kim to focus. "Tell me, Kim—what did you find?"

She cupped her face in her hands as new tears poured out. "They killed them—they killed them all," she cried. "My mom—she wouldn't come out of her room—cried for a week. Those scenes on the TV—that little boy, his son, saluting the casket." She pulled her hands away and her eyes were black smudges trailing down her cheeks. "They took them all from us, Walk—JFK, Doctor King, and Bobby."

I handed Kim a napkin, gestured. "Your makeup." She took it. "Peter," I said, "tell me about Peter."

"He's one of them. His files—he hid them you know—after. But I knew where to look—I'm onto the phony's game. I found them and I read them, and you know what? He tracks people down. He finds them and makes them disappear. My God, Walk—he kills them."

"Peter?"

"Him and his righteous friends—answering to some higher power. Last year, they killed that guy—the Beatles road manager. Remember that story in the news? About the guy killed in a stand-off with the L.A. police. His name was Mal Evans—a gentle giant. He was in Peter's files. They killed him—Peter did—he and his cop friends. And everything they collected from his apartment—all his Beatles notebooks—it all conveniently disappeared from the evidence room."

"You're sure?"

"I can read, can't I? And you know something else? We're all in those files—you, me, Tommy, Mr. Scanlon. They want something they think we have and they won't stop until they get it."

"Okay, Kim—okay. We've got to get you out of there—away from him. Do you have a place you can go? Somewhere safe?"

Kim blew her nose into a napkin. "—not running."

"What?"

"You heard me. I'm not running. I've got his files and something else—a phone number. I think it's a number for them."

"Them?"

"The bad guys. The number's written on a dollar bill Peter framed and hung over our nightstand. All that time—right under my nose."

I pointed out to her that the number could be anything or nothing at all.

"Maybe—but maybe not. I'm not dumb you know. I notice things—put things together. There's that pyramid—on a dollar—that symbol—the Eye of Providence. It was in the files. It means something to them."

"The files, Kim—where are they?"

"Someplace safe."

"What are you planning to do with them?"

"Take them to the cops—to a lawyer—anyone who'll listen."

"Not the cops. You said yourself he has friends there."

"Fine—a lawyer then, or a judge. But first I'm going to call that number. I'm calling it tonight."

"Not a good idea," I said.

"Why not?"

"If they're as dangerous as you say—"

"Bullshit! I've been afraid for seven years—no more. I'm calling the number."

"Fine. But not from your place—not Peter's."

"Fine. Where then?"

"Pick a place—a payphone—anywhere—just not there. Don't go back there, period."

Customers were beginning to straggle in—dinner time. Tommy and Jules would be getting home soon. I glanced at my watch.

Kim noticed. "You're done with me," she said.

"No—sorry. It's just that I have to go."

"So go."

I got up. "Kim, you're a good person—a beautiful person." I kissed her cheek. "You are loved and don't forget it."

She cracked a fragile smile and waved me gone.

I left Kim intending to go straight to Tommy's. I would make things right with him and Jules. I would tell them everything. *Everything.* I checked the time again—figured I had just enough room for an interim stop.


I GAVE A QUICK wave as I rushed past Jimmy at his easel and found Esse on her kitchen chair.

"Esse," I said, "what do you know about this?"

She looked at what I held in my hand. "Why it's a dolla, boy. You trying to be funny?"

I pointed to the pyramid and the eye within it.

She raised her arms—two hands forming a triangle. "The Eye of Providence," she said, "the all- seeing eye."

"A symbol of the Freemasons," I said, "—the secret society."

"Oh—that's the phooey they'd have you believe, but the real truth ain't them Knights Templar or Founding Fathers. It's the enemy within."

"What's that?"

"The underworld, boy—the occult. It's what runs things."

She reached out for my hand and held it tightly in hers. Closing her eyes, she trembled. With her eyes shut tight, she uttered, "Darkness descending."

*Kim*, I thought. She's going back to that house.

"Esse, I have to go."

"Yes, boy—you go. You go careful."

## OMAHA/DECEMBER 9, 1977

Inside an unremarkable house in a middle class Omaha neighborhood, a man in his mid-sixties answered the front door and another man, fortyish, stepped inside. The older man fell back into his chair and picked up his half-finished glass of bourbon while the younger closed the front window blinds. Finishing his drink, the older man reached to switch on a nearby clock radio—set to static. He adjusted the volume up slightly and asked, "So what do we have?"

The younger man spoke for the first time. "A foot soldier's been compromised."

"Where?"

"West Division—L.A."

"Go on—"

"At 5:27pm Pacific Time today, we received a call from his assigned line—a payphone near his residence."

"So the number dialed and the outgoing line matched up?"

"Correct. The caller was asked for the code. The call was disconnected."

"Who's end?"

"Theirs. A second call was made from the same line two minutes later at 5:29pm. The caller was again asked for the code. A woman spoke. She said, "Who is this?" The call was immediately disconnected—our end."

"A girl. Do we know who it might be?"

"In all likelihood, we believe it to be his live-in, a Kimberly Reiser."

"And the agent?"

"Peter Hartford."

"Pedigree?"

"Dallas legion."

"I see."

"For that reason, we wanted to check with you."

The older man rolled the melted cubes inside his glass then set it down. "Contain it."

Without a word, the younger man proceeded down the hall and out to the garage where a CB radio awaited his three-word command, "King and Queen." He returned to the living room not more than a minute later and addressed his superior. "We'll need a new code number, sir."

The older man stood from his chair and went to a bookshelf. "The prior?" he asked.

"*The Great Gatsby*."

"Yes—of course." The old man took a random paperback from the shelf—*Catcher In The Rye*. "Never much liked this novel," he said. He opened the book to the title page and put his finger on the Library of Congress serial number.

The young man said, "Yes, sir—*Catcher In The Rye* it is."

---

I DROPPED MY BIKE around the corner and sprinted along the darkened sidewalk sure I'd recognize the house when I saw it. I'd been to Peter and Kim's place just once before. I saw what I thought to be the house and remembered now the iron bars on the front door and windows—overkill even for that neighborhood. Nearing the drive, a shape appeared out of the dark and brushed past. Startled, I thought—*Brandt?*

I called out. "Detective Brandt?"

The figure stopped and turned—came forward into the light. "Walker," he said, as surprised as I was.

"Detective Brandt, what are you doing here?"

"Out for a walk," he said.

"You live around here?"

He hesitated, "I could ask you the same. What brings you around here?"

"Going to see a friend," I said.

"Yeah?" he asked.

I pointed at the house. "She lives right here—I think."

Brandt stood silent as he looked toward the house. A chill clawed inside me. I said, "Well, good seeing you—," and started for the house.

Brandt stepped into my path. "Hold on."

Just then, headlights and the *bleet-bleet* of a siren ripped through the night. A squad car blew past us and skidded to a stop in front of the house—its red and blue strobes spinning. Two cops rushed the front door—Kim's door. A second car arrived seconds later, nearly clipping us where we stood. A cop popped out with his gun trained on us. He was easing closer when he recognized Brandt. "Detective," he said. Holstering his gun, he half-smiled. "Isn't Homicide usually the second call?"

Brandt went to him and they shook hands. I overheard Brandt say he'd heard the shots fired call on the radio and was in the area. Hearing that, I made a dash for Kim's. Brandt gave chase and grabbed me forcibly by my arm. He motioned to the cop who rushed over. "We're going to need Mr. Walker to stay right here," Brandt told the cop. The cop nodded and planted himself between me and the house.

I watched from the street as Brandt showed his badge to a cop at the door and entered the house. I got a sickening feeling that Brandt knew exactly what he'd find inside.

One of the cops exited the house and came over to us. "Who's this?" he asked, pointing at me.

"Nobody," the cop responded. "What are we looking at?"

"Murder-suicide," the cop said, "cut and dried."

*Kim!*

I rushed toward the house again, but the cop stopped me—pushing me against his car. "Don't move," he ordered. Deciding he needed to see the gore for himself, he stuffed me into the backseat of his squad car. When he disappeared into the house, I opened the unlocked car door and bolted for my bike.

BACK AT MY PLACE I quickly stuffed what clothes I could into my duffle. I saw my helmet still lodged in the wall over my bed and pried it free. I picked up my guitar case—emptied it of my bank roll—and left out the back.

I pushed my bike a ways to make a quiet exit. Running alongside, I picked up speed and jumped aboard. I dropped the clutch and the bike rung to life. I gunned the throttle.

Instantly, headlights appeared ahead—coming fast. I leaned in and stayed my course. We sped by each other on that lit street—him seeing me and me seeing him.

I didn't stop—I kept going—but not out of fear of Brandt and his brotherhood. I kept going because it was Tommy—my friend, my comrade. I kept going because I was afraid that in my eyes, he'd see what would hurt him most—my betrayal.

## TOMMY'S APARTMENT/WEST ALAMEDA/DECEMBER 9, 1977

Jules was starting dinner when Tommy came in. He was late.

She called to him, "Spaghetti alright, babe?"

When she got no answer, she turned, saw Tommy's face, and immediately took the pot off the burner. Leaning against the range, she said to him, "Come here." Tommy just looked away. Concerned, she went to him. "What is it? What's wrong?"

Tommy stared blankly. "I went by your work."

Jules took his hands, trying desperately to read him. "You did? Why?"

Tommy stiffened. "To talk to your boss."

"Rand? About what?" She took his arm and turned him to face her. "Tommy, tell me what's going on."

"I just wanted to talk to him."

"About what?"

"Nothing—okay. It doesn't matter now anyway."

"Tommy, you're not making any sense."

"Forget it," he said, "you weren't there—okay—so I came home. I'm here now."

Jules waited for more. Instead, Tommy spun away fingering his top button. "I'm gonna change."

He went to the bedroom, opened a drawer, and stared at the folded shirts there. In his head, he wrestled with Walk blowing by him on the street just minutes ago. Anger rose up inside of him.

Jules leaned on the counter, summoning her strength as she relit the burner. She knew it was time. When Tommy came back out, she said to him, "We've got to talk about Walk."

"What about him?"

"First, tell me we're okay." She turned off the stove again, moved to the table. "Please—sit with me."

Tommy put a white-knuckle hold on a chair back. "What about Walk?"

"I don't know exactly," she started.

Anger overwhelmed Tommy. He said, "You said we need to talk—so talk. Just say it."

Jules stumbled on her words. "It's just that—you were right—when you said he'd never find another girl—because of me." She felt the heat of Tommy's eyes on her. "I think—I think Walk puts himself between us."

"What the shit does that mean—between us?"

Jules spilled what fell short of any explanation. "He loves you Tommy—you know he does. He emulates you. But he lives in your shadow."

Tommy barked, "My shadow? I never put him in any damn shadow."

"I know you haven't—I didn't say that right. It's just that Walk is confused, twisted up—you know. He needs so desperately for something of his own."

Tommy lifted and slammed the chair to the floor. "TELL ME!" he shouted, "Tell me what it is that he wants for his own. I'd really like to know what the fuck that is."

Jules went to Tommy wrapping her arms around him. He stood cold and rigid. He spoke low into the crown of her head—into hair that smelled like rain. He said, "Where's my shirt?"

Jules tilted her face up to Tommy's. "What are you talking about? What shirt?"

Tommy pulled away. He rushed back to the bedroom dresser. He tore through the drawers. He flung open the closet grabbing handfuls of clothes and threw them aside. He ripped the empty clothes bar from its anchors. Turning to Jules, he growled, "Tell—me—where—my—shirt—is."

"Tommy!" Jules cried out. "What is wrong with you?"

"What's wrong? Walk. My shirt. You tell me what's wrong."

Jules went into the bathroom and turned over the hamper. She came back with Tommy's shirt. She threw it at him and stood, arms crossed. "I don't know what you think is going on here but whatever it is—you're wrong."

"I'm wrong? Really? But you and Walk—that's not wrong?"

Jules was crushed, stripped. Fighting back tears, she pleaded with Tommy. "Don't say it," she said biting her lip. "Don't you dare say those words. Because if you say it, you can never take it back."

"Never?" Tommy clarified, "Well, consider me so advised." Then he said it.

"Are you fucking him? Are you fucking Walk?"

## Chapter Twenty

I<small>T WAS MID-MORNING</small> of the next day when I parked out front. Tucking my helmet under an arm, I entered the house quietly and came upon her in the kitchen.

She jumped. "Ah—Oh!—oh my gosh. You nearly scared me half to death."

I moved to her and gave my mom a hug.

"You didn't call. I didn't know you were coming. Why didn't you call?"

"I wanted to surprise you."

She finally let go of me. "Well—you sure did—don't you know you shouldn't sneak up on an old lady like that?"

"You're not old, mom."

"I am too," she fussed with her hair, "—just look at me."

"You really ought to lock your doors," I told her.

She wasn't listening. "You hungry?"

"Always." I put my helmet down on the table and pulled out a chair. I watched her make me a sandwich and wondered how many times she performed that simple act of love for me. "Aren't you having one?" I asked. Again, she wasn't listening. She cut the stacked bread corner to corner, arranged some chips and some grapes on the plate and set it down in front of me. "What can I get you to drink?"

"Just water."

She stood at the fridge. "You want soda? I have Pepsi, 7-UP."

"Water's fine."

She poured me a glass and hovered over me, watching me eat.

"Grab a seat, mom, you're making me nervous."

"You look good," she said, "your face is clear."

I just smiled.

"Well, you do—you look good. I haven't seen you in a while."

"I know—sorry. I should come more often."

"Don't be silly—no, it's fine really—I know you're busy. You got your life there and that's how it's supposed to be. I'm fine. Really."

I asked, "How was your Thanksgiving? Aunt Sheri good? Gordon still doing his stamps?"

"They're all fine. Emily wasn't there—she's got a serious guy. They're hoping for a Christmas proposal."

"Is that right? Well—good for Emily."

"She's a sweetheart, that girl. So, you haven't said, how's Tommy? And Jules?"

"They're alright—all good."

"And will she be getting a ring anytime soon?"

"I wouldn't know."

"Well—he best get a move on with that one, she's a keeper."

"Yeah. Jules is—best."

"And you? Are you seeing anyone?"

"Uh, yeah—actually."

"Does she have a name?"

"Melissa. Her name's Melissa."

The dryer buzzed in the laundry and I was suddenly alone in the kitchen. I went to the drawer where she kept the address book. In the back was a paper scrap with his name and number. I tucked the scrap into my pocket.

She came up behind me and slipped a ski cap over my head. "Early Christmas," she smiled, "I wasn't sure if I'd see you."

I pulled off the cap and had a look at it. I put it back on. "Thanks, mom."

She stepped back to admire it—me. "Looks good on you. Maybe you'll actually wear it—not like that helmet of yours."

"Mom," I said reaching for her, "I've got to go."

We hugged. "I love you."

"I love you too."


I LEFT MY MOM'S with no particular destination in mind. No, that's not entirely true—I had my dad's phone number. I rode north, decided only to keep the crashing coastline on my left. I didn't know how far or how lost was enough to avoid Brandt's reach.

My body found strange solace on the bike—my hands firm on the grips, my wrist flexed full throttle, the heels of my boots resting easy on the pegs. My back pressed snug against the duffle strapped behind me, the vibration of the road beneath me and the warm sun on my face—it all soothed me to the bone. But in my head—chaos—my every deception a hot-poker memory. I wondered what Tommy thought of me abandoning him like that—and what Jules would think of me. I thought of Kim—*poor Kim*—could she really be gone?

At Ventura, I continued north on California Highway One through Carpinteria and Santa Barbara. I spent my first night on the beach at Goleta. Next was the fishing village of Morro Bay where I got a room for the night. From my window, I watched the evening mist gather around the mystic rock island anchored in the bay as if splashed down from some heavenly summit. I listened to the sea lions sing their siren song beneath the yellow moon and it drew me outside in the middle of my sleepless night. Restless as the tide, I went to the water's edge and felt the pull of its swirling blackness at my feet—pulling me in—pulling me down. In the morning, I ate my eggs among the locals and watched the fishermen prepare their boats for the day. I left Morro Bay, pointing my bike due east toward the rising sun and Bakersfield.

The sun was high in the sky when I passed beneath the Bakersfield sign and into downtown. It struck me that Bakersfield, with its jumble of historic stone buildings and green spaces alongside lifeless high-rises and hot pavement, didn't know whether it wanted to be a town or a big city. Cruising along 18th, I stopped in front of one of the more striking older buildings that caught my eye. The sign out front read Masonic temple #224. I climbed the stairs to the grand wooden door that was locked. Carved into the limestone above the door was the symbol of the Freemasons—a corner square and a compass forming a loose triangle. Inside it was an eye—the same eye as within the pyramid on a dollar bill.

My next stop was the Beale Memorial Public Library—an architectural example of one of the city's boorishly brutal new builds. Inside, I idled in front of the card catalogue cabinets without a clue where to start or even how to use the damn Dewey Decimal System. I noticed I was being watched so I walked right up to the guy behind the counter. He fit the part of librarian—glasses, long face, severely parted hair, button-down sweater the color of dried grass with patches on the elbows. He greeted me with, "Finding what you need?"

"You got any books about Freemasons or the Eye of Providence?"

"Which one?" he asked.

I held out my hands making the shape of the triangle—like Esse did.

I followed him to the reference section where he pulled several books saying, "These should get you started."

I grabbed a seat and spent the next hour flipping through the books. The Eye of God and its roots in the divine gaze dated back to the second century BC in the writings of the church. The eye was often depicted within a triangle—the three sides representing the Trinity. In the 1700's, the symbol was adopted by the Bavarian Secret Society and early Masonic movements. I read that these secretive groups were founded on the principles of enlightenment and forbidden knowledge. These groups were often referred to as the Unseen Hand for their role in orchestrating world events like revolutions and wars. The groups and the conspiracy theories surrounding them survived right up until current day. The Illuminati is one such group said to include Presidents of the United States as members. These groups can have a dark side with leanings toward cults and occultism. Some promoted the idea of a new world order made possible through use of mind control. I noted that among the many conspiracy theories tied to these groups, the JFK assassination seemed the most prevalent.

I'd seen enough—so there was something to all this. But still, I found nothing related to the sunglasses unless you count medieval crystal balls or black obsidian mirrors as possible predecessors. And I was no closer to knowing who or what exactly was behind Brandt and his goon squad.

I left the books lying on the table and headed toward the door. Mr. Librarian cleared his throat as I passed so I obliged him by detouring to his counter. He motioned to a stack of books before him. "I took the liberty of pulling some recommendations in the category of fiction," he said.

I read the first title aloud. "*The Nine Unknown*."

"Published in 1923 by Talbot Mundy," he added.

"Okay?" I said.

"Mundy's novel is based upon the premise that there exists a bank of knowledge or secrets that, in the wrong hands, would pose a danger to mankind. The nine men in the story were entrusted with preserving and keeping safe the nine books of secrets."

"Got it. And this book?"

"*The Morning of the Magicians* was originally written in French by two journalists. It was translated to English and released in 1968."

"What's it about?"

"I couldn't say, precisely. But reading the summary, it appears to be a bible of sorts for conspiracy theorists. Apparently, it introduces the occult as pervasive in these beliefs and the keystone of world order."

"The occult, huh? You believe in that stuff?" I asked.

"Me?—for heaven's sake, no."

"You should," I said, and walked out.

FROM BAKERSFIELD, I CAUGHT Hwy 5 north and passed through the towns of Wasco and Lost Hills. I took 198 east and arrived in Visalia by evening where I pulled into a roadside taco stand. I sat under a massive fig tree at the corner of the lot and ate my tacos. Before long, I had company—a stray dog trotted over. He was a mutt that looked to have some hound in him with his long ears and sad eyes. He reminded me of Gil at the Plaza. I tossed him a taco scrap and he showed his appreciation by curling up next to me. I gave him a good scratch and he'd nudge me for more as soon as I'd stop. I ended up spending the night under that tree with my new friend. Before sleep came to me, my thoughts returned home—to Tommy and Jules—to the times we'd had together.

"Think quick," Jules called as she hurled a piece of toast at my head.

I snatched it out of the air frisbee style. I broke off a crusty corner and called back to her, "Open wide!"

Jules stuck out her strawberry tongue—daring me. I let it fly and the chunk careened off her forehead. Tommy lunged to pick it off the floor and popped it into his mouth.

"I can't believe you just did that," Jules said.

"What?" Tommy said, "There's starving children in China."

Jules wiped the smear of butter from her brow. "Not you," she said, "I can't believe Walk threw that at me."

"You threw first," I said.

"What's your point?" she teased. Jules plunked another two slices into the toaster. "You best not ever do that again," she said to me crossing one eye, "—I could have lost my good eye."

"Not likely with your mouth such a big target," I said.

Tommy grinned in amusement at our peppered exchange.

Jules pointed to her forehead. "Does this look like my mouth to you? Admit it—you missed."

"My throw was perfect. You moved."

"No—you missed."

"No—you moved."

Tommy grabbed the toast still in my hand and jammed it into his mouth. "You lose."

"Know what I'm thinking?" Jules said suddenly. "I'm thinking we need a dog."

Tommy was quick with, "We don't need a dog. We've got Walk."

"Hey," I said, "wasn't me eating off the floor."

"A shelter dog," Jules said, "—one that needs a home and someone to cuddle and play with."

"You've got me for that," Tommy said. He turned to me, grinning. "She's got me for that."

I gave him two thumbs up.

"Yes, but I gave up on house breaking you a long time ago," she said to him.

That was the end of the doggie discussion that night but for weeks after, I tried to talk Tommy into surprising Jules with a puppy. He wouldn't go for it.

Huddled under our tree, I scratched Gil behind the ears. "You wanna go home with me, boy—huh? You wanna meet Jules?" Gil raised his head momentarily then dropped his wet muzzle back to my thigh. "No?—alright. You'd like her though."

I WOKE TO THE sound of gravel popping beneath the tires of work trucks pulling into the convenience store across the street. Gil and I watched the migrant workers file in and come out with armloads of Clamato Juice, Gatorade, bruised plantains and packages of factory-made sweet rolls. When Gil looked up at me and whined, I told him to go on. He trotted across the street and took up his panhandling with the pickers. The field workers left as quickly as they'd come—packed like prisoners into the backs of flatbed trucks. I walked across to the store and bought a few items myself. I ate some jerky and a banana outside with Gil watching. I washed it down with an apple juice. I stuffed two more bananas and a can of Hawaiian Punch into my pack for later. I gave Gil the rest of my jerky and was on my way.

There's no better place in the world to disappear than in California's Central Valley—the nation's Salad Bowl. There's not an interested soul around—just miles and miles of black irrigation tubes cannoning water across forever rows of green under a sky like a cowboy cliché. It was to be my everlasting summer—on the run—but from what exactly? Brandt? Or my own conscience?

I SAT ALONE AT the counter of a roadside diner in Fresno shuffling through scraps of songs written on whatever was handy. I'd been writing—or trying to. I pulled from the pile a photograph—high school seniors.

"Coffee?"

The waitress stood over me waiving a quarter pot and a mug.

"Sure."

She poured—went away—came back and dropped a menu. "Whenever you're ready, hon."

Holding the photograph, I studied my eighteen-year-old self and tried to recall what I was thinking at the moment when the shutter clicked. Me sandwiched between Jules and Tommy—the third wheel. In my eyes, I saw the void that was always there—an emptiness I tried to fill with pieces and parts outside of myself. What I liked—how I talked—even how I dressed. I went back to that stupid mall and bought the same shirt as Tommy—the one with *too fast to live too young to die* across the back. Tommy had one and I had to have one too—a shirt I was too afraid to wear in public for fear of being found out. As what?—a copycat—a follower—a fake? And I didn't stop there. I hit Cody Vale with that pitch, not for Tommy but my own jealousy of Cody kissing Jules.

When the sunglasses came into my life, I had my chance to finally experience what Tommy had with Jules. And I got so caught up that I couldn't see that it was wrong for me to know Jules that way—her breath in my ear, the warmth of her back to mine, the rhythm of her. The sunglasses wanted to show me more—the shape of her as she undressed, stepped from the shower, or crawled toward the pillow. But I wouldn't go there. When the sunglasses tempted, I'd pull back—tune out—and wake up alone in my own bed.

It was that way not just with Jules, but with all the women that came to me in my golden slumbers—with one exception. Melissa and I had started innocently enough—in what I thought was a dream. But soon enough, I was going back for more—shadowing Baros and taking what was his. I'm not proud of it, but it's done. My one and only girlfriend—and, let's face it, even that wasn't real.

"Decided yet?"

"Ah—yeah, could I get two eggs over easy, some bacon, and do you have hash browns?"

"That's a number four."

"Okay."

"You want toast with that?"

"Huh?"

"It comes with toast—white or rye?"

"No. No toast."

## Chapter Twenty-One

I GOT MY FIRST motorcycle, a Honda trail 70, when I was fourteen. My dad got it for me. Mom never liked it. Like so many things in life—it scared her. That bike was my everything. I'd ride it all day long and even dream about it at night. There was one dream I'd have again and again, and it always ended the same. In it, I'd be riding with Jackie Kennedy on back. She wore that pale pink suit and she'd be saying—*Hurry, please hurry*. As dreams go, I could never get my bike to go fast—fast enough—because every time we'd arrive too late. She and I would watch from a grassy hill as his car rounded the corner—like in a parade. I'd look at her and point out the blood on her pink suit and she'd say—*Yes, I know, I want them to see what they've done to Jack*.

Every night, I'd go to bed hoping that, just once, in my dream, we'd make it there on time.

IN FRESNO, I TALKED to a man about a gig at a bar there. His name was Phil and he told me right off that the bar was his livelihood, but music was his passion. For some reason, he asked to see my guitar. I told him I didn't have one—said I didn't know getting a gig would be so easy. Phil reminded me that I didn't have a gig yet. I asked him where I could buy a guitar and he told me there was a music store near the university. I rode there straight away and found a gem—a Gibson J-50. I went back to Phil's. He seemed surprised to see me back. He said to show him the guitar. I did. He looked it over like a man buying a horse. He told me he loved guitar but couldn't play—said his fingers were too fat. He asked me if I knew anything by Dylan. I told him I did and asked if there was a particular song that he wanted to hear. He answered with what he figured would surely stump me. "It's a Dylan bootleg," he said, "—untitled and never officially released but affectionately called by his fans 'Rock Me Mamma.'"

I asked for my guitar back and I played him his song. When I'd finished, he stuck out his thick hand. "Tips and all the beer you can drink."

"Deal," I said.

"What do I call you?"

I thought about that for a second. "Bucko," I said.

"Bucko it is," he said and slapped a hand to his thigh.

After the audition, I got myself a room for the night at a motel just up the road. All I had were hundreds, so the check-in clerk got an eyeful. Along with my change, he included a card for a ten percent discount at a restaurant he highly recommended. He said to be sure to tell them who sent me. He even wrote his name on the card so I wouldn't forget—Vince Gumm.

I grabbed my guitar and duffle and climbed the stairs to the room. The water was hot, but the pressure was crap. I used the tiny bar soap on my body and hair. I lingered in the steam until the water ran cold. Wrapping a towel around my waist, I pulled the blanket off the bed and laid across the cool sheets.

I WOKE AROUND SIX with my stomach rumbling. I pulled on my jeans and a flannel shirt and headed over to Phil's early. My set wasn't until eight. Phil saw me come in and set me up at the bar with a Bud and a bowl of pretzels.

I was on my fourth beer when my time came at Big Phil's mic. It could have been me but every face in the joint looked blitzed out of their minds. A good ol' boy stumbled up to request the first song of the night—"Free Bird". It would be a night of covers—the more obscure requests coming from my host and employer behind the bar. A couple of hours in, a lone voice called out for "I Am The Walrus". It was the only Beatles tune requested that night, and a strange request at that. I stood to see who'd called for it, but the face was lost in the crowd. The song was one I'd researched with lyrics something like—I am he and you are me as we are all together. *The sunglasses.* I didn't play it—just moved on to the next request.

Things wound down a little after 2 a.m. I'd exhausted the entirety of what I knew from the Eagles, The Dirt Band, Allman Brothers, Skynyrd, and CCR catalogs. After one last beer with Phil, he handed me my tips and smiled, "Same time tomorrow." I said my good nights to the staff and rode my bike the short distance back to the motel—my body screaming for sleep.

WHAT I FOUND WAITING for me in my motel room ripped me in half with an overwhelming sense of panic and loss. I'll describe the scene for you as I'd pieced it together based on what I'd walked into.

A skinny greaseball with a ponytail strolled up the stairs with a full ring of keys jangling from his western belt. Leaning against the rail, he looked out over the parking lot to confirm the absence of a certain motorbike. He took a last drag from his cigarette and flicked the butt over the rail. He shuffled his bony ass to room 207. In the light of the yellow bug-bulb, he fingered the numbered key and unlocked the door. The lights were off inside but his hand knew right where to find the switch and the crooked lamp on the fiberboard dresser came to life. He went straight to the bathroom to check the sink and cabinet for pills or drugs. He found only a toothbrush. He moved to my duffle laying on a chair and dumped its contents on the bed. He smiled as he counted the rolls of cash—all hundreds—and stuffed them into his pockets. He saw a notebook on the bedside table and brought it back into the bathroom where he took a shit. While at it, he read what looked to him to be poems. He stood, rolled the notebook and stuffed it into the front of his jeans. He didn't flush. Back at the bed, he rummaged once more through the clothes. He found a guitar pick in a pair of jeans. He picked up a pair of rolled socks and thought it felt odd. Unrolling them, he found a pair of sunglasses, which he promptly pocketed. He left the room without locking the door. Later, he'd suggest that maybe the guest left it that way. He'd offer a mock apology and point to the posted sign—*Management not responsible for lost or stolen items.*

By my reckoning, this greaseball had a name—Vince Gumm.

The motel office was dark and deserted, so I went back to my room and pulled the chair over to the window to keep watch. *Fuck!*

THE DAYLIGHT STREAMING THROUGH the window woke me. I went out and banged on the sliding window at the office. There was someone new in the chair—not Vince. The new guy yelled to me without turning around, "Drop it in the slot." I banged again even harder. Still with his back to me he called, "Just leave the key in the slot."

I went around to the side door and pulled the sonofabitch out of his chair. "Where's Vince?" The guy collapsed through my hands onto the floor. Surprised, I stood back. It was then I saw the wheelchair beside the desk. I helped him back into the chair.

"What's your name?" I asked him.

"Marty."

"Marty—I'm sorry."

He just stared at me.

"Marty—I need to know where Vince is."

"He's not on 'till tonight. He covers the five to midnight."

I figured with all my cash there was no way in hell Vince was coming in tonight. "Where is he now—where does he live?"

"Huh?—outside of town somewhere—I think."

"Do you have a number for him—an address?"

"Maybe—yeah—we should." Marty flipped through the Rolodex. "Here," he said.

I pulled the card—it had only a number. I set it by the phone. "Call him."

Marty dialed, waited, looked at me. "There's no answer."

I took out the business card Vince had given me when I checked in. I held it up for Marty to read. "This place," I said, "—where can I find Parson's."

"It's a restaurant," he said.

"And—"

"I've never eaten there but it's supposed to be good."

"Where is it, Marty?"

"Huh? Oh—it's on Burlington out near the Central Hardware."

"And that's where from here?"

"Oh—you make a left outta here onto the interstate and another left on Valleyside. Parson's will be about a quarter mile up Burlington."

"Right or left on Burlington?"

"Lemme think—it'd be a right."

"They open for breakfast?"

"No—don't think so."

I took Vince's card back and gave Marty my room key.

"Oh—okay," he said.


I FOUND PARSON'S. The place was locked up—dead quiet. I went across the street and into an Eat-Rite. From a window booth, I kept an eye on Parson's lot. The waitress dropped off a menu. I looked it over and panicked for a split second. I dug into my jeans and pulled out my tip money from last night—thirty-three dollars. And I had a pair of twenties in my wallet. Seventy-three dollars to my name.

The wall on the clock read ten o'clock. Still no sign of life at Parson's. I called the waitress over. I pointed across the street. "Do you know when they open?"

"What? Parson's? Around four, I guess." She stood over me. "You want to see our lunch menu?"

"No."

"More water?"

"No. Thanks. Hey, can I ask you something? You wouldn't happen to know a Vince Gumm?"

"Gumm, you say? Nope—can't say that I do."

I figured I couldn't hang any more without ordering something, so I left. As I climbed onto my bike, a patrol car parked alongside me. I pulled my helmet on and tightened the chin strap. The cops got out of their car. The younger one looked at me and gave me a half wave. Inside, they sat in the booth I'd just vacated.

I tooled around the town until four o'clock. More and more, I figured Parson's was a long shot. Sure enough, the hostess didn't know Vince. She said the owner should be in shortly and that he might. I waited outside around the back where the employees parked. A guy pulled up fast in a beater and jumped out. He hustled to the back door, took a last drag from his cigarette and reached for the door handle.

"Hey," I said, "got a minute?"

"No, man—late for work."

I held out a twenty.

He looked at me—the cash. "What?"

"Do you know a Vince—Vince Gumm?"

He reached for the twenty. "Gumm? Don't know any Gumm."

I pulled back the bill. "How about a Vince?"

"Nope. Don't know no Vince either." He shuffled his feet. "Look, man—I gotta get in there."

I handed him the twenty. "One more question. Where would you go to blow off steam if you were overflowing with the green?"

The guy smiled greasy as his shoes. "That's an easy one—strip club."

I waited for more, requiring of him another second of his limited attention span.

"Clem's out 180 toward the airport. Exit at Peach and head south."


THE PARKING LOT AT Clementine's was packed with pick-ups, work vans and assorted muscle cars sporting more primer than paint. The fatty at the door looked me over and said, "Ten buck cover and a two-drink minimum."

I told him I was meeting someone and could I just take a look around inside.

He chuckled. "Be my guest. Ten bucks."

I counted four stages, and not a front row seat to be had. I scanned the backs of heads looking for a ponytail. I made my rounds in the dark dogging drunks, drink trays, and double D's. I climbed steps to the upper level and stood at the brass rail to get a better view. Trouble broke out on stage three where a Mexican girl was dancing. Two guys were wrestling at her feet. Fatty from the door was there in a heartbeat to break it up.

I stopped a passing waitress. She was thin with small pointy tits and bruises on her thighs. I leaned in so she could hear me over the music. "Do you know a Vince?"

"No," she said. "What are you drinking?"

"I'm good," I told her.

"Look—you have to be drinking or they'll throw you out."

"Budweiser."

She came back and handed me my beer. "Five dollars."

I gave her a ten. She stuffed it into her G-string and walked away.

I nursed my beer for a long while with no sign of Vince. I set my bottle down preparing to leave when somebody asked, "You looking for Vince?"

I turned to see another waitress—a pretty girl I'd noticed on stage earlier. "Yeah," I said.

She pointed to a section of red velvet curtain near the back of the club. She picked up my empty and handed it to me. "You're going to need that, and me, to get back there. Follow me."

She paused outside the curtain. "They're watching," she said, "you're going to have to pay me."

I pulled out my last twenty. "This enough?"

She took it and peeled back the curtain. She led me down the hall. "He's in there," she pointed.

"Why you helping me?"

She looked at me with sympathetic eyes. "I heard you play—the other night."

"Is there a back way out of here?"

She pointed to a back door. "There'll be muscle on the other side." She turned and was gone.

Vince was in there—a girl grinding on his lap. When he saw me, he stood and knocked her to the floor. I backed him up against the wall and the girl ran out.

"What's your problem?" he slurred.

I spun him around and pulled his wallet—plump with my hundreds. I took the bills and tossed the wallet.

"Where's the rest of it?"

"What are you talking about, man?"

I put my knee hard into his thigh. He collapsed but caught himself with the chair on the way down. I heard a commotion in the hall, so I grabbed Vince and drug him under the side curtain into the next space over. There was a guy in there getting head. He looked at us and went right on with her. I put Vince on the ground—muffled by my boot on his neck. I heard Fatty and the girl. The curtain parted slightly—they didn't see us—the curtain closed. I gave it a five-count and stuck my head out into the hall in time to catch Fatty heading out the back—Vince's girl trailing behind with her bare ass to me. I hauled off and kicked Vince in the head. I squatted and hoisted him over my shoulder in a fireman's carry. I walked right out the front door with him on my back. If it's not naked and gyrating, nobody's noticing nothing.

When I shook Vince awake in the parking lot, he couldn't remember where he'd parked. "What do you drive?"

"A P-Pinto," he stammered.

I took his keys and administered another swift kick to his head—lights out.

I found the car—my notebook on the front seat, sunglasses on the rearview and three rolls of my cash in the glove box. He must have stashed the rest—a few grand—at his place. He'd need it for his medical bills. I used my pitching arm to launch his keys far enough he'd never find them.

I left Fresno for good. Two hours south, I pulled off the road and took the sunglasses from my jacket. Holding them again after having lost them, I realized the great significance of what I held in my hands. I knew then that I needed to be a better caretaker—or find someone who would be.

## ERIC CLAPTON'S ESTATE/WESTCHESTER/APRIL 1969

George sat at the Clapton's breakfast table alternating his attention between his coffee and his cigarette. Eric was there, along with longtime friend, Klaus Voorman. It was a casual affair. Another musician and mutual friend, Alistair Whittacker, was staying over as well but left early and well before breakfast that morning.

The night before, after the others had gone to bed, George entrusted Alistair with a certain item; told only to keep it safe and out of reach. George had originally intended to give the item to Klaus, but decided Klaus was too close and too sympathetic toward John.

Earlier that morning, George sat alone in the garden with one of Eric's guitars. His mind flashed through the past few difficult months and the Get Back sessions—the bickering, Paul's overbearing ambition, John and Yoko's antics, the low whispers in the control room. Then there was George's drug bust and his own frayed nerves. And yet, as the sun came over the rise George couldn't help but feel a sense of renewal—if not for the band, then at least for the relationship between his boyhood friends. As far as George was concerned, the object at the heart of the distrust and wedge between John and Paul was now gone—safe and out of reach.

As the long-absent sun warmed his face, a calm fell over George and a song poured out. It began as a delicate guitar piece, tumbling down. What followed were the words that would be the title of perhaps his greatest masterpiece—"Here Comes The Sun". The band's long cold lonely winter was over. Or was it?

## Chapter Twenty-Two

I FOUND MYSELF SOUTHBOUND on highway 99, again near Bakersfield. I wasn't ready to risk Los Angeles so I circled around it on the 210 through Pasadena. I continued south past San Bernardino then caught the 10 into Palm Springs. Uncle Steve owned a second dealership there run by a college friend of his. I'd met Bill once and thought about talking to him about a job—but no—too risky. Besides, Palm Springs was far too pretentious and plastic for me—so I headed west toward Carlsbad and the coast.

So began a long stretch of days spent along the beaches south of L.A. Mornings, I'd play my guitar and write in the room I was renting. I'd nap afternoons near or on the beach. I'd eat at any one of the food shacks dotting the coastline at Dana Point, Capistrano, and Doheny Beach.

Most evenings at sunset, you'd find me on the sand watching the sun go down through my shades. I'd sit transfixed, hoping the universe would reveal its truths and point a way back home for me. But the only golden haze was on the horizon and my answers never came. When the tide would chase me off, I'd find myself a barstool and hide behind my shades waiting for lesser secrets to be revealed—the local goings on, the dirty deeds. I scouted bars that featured live music and would work in a guitar lesson or take the stage myself to float something new I'd written. It was a lonely existence.

During those long days spent on the beach, old memories swept in like the tide—taking me back to when Tommy, Jules and I were new. I thought about that time on Topanga Beach when Jules taught me how to surf. Over and over, I'd tumble into the waves—lost and disoriented—only to have Jules pull me from the water. She'd smile in her way to let me know she wanted me to try again. And for her, I would—I did. And I got it—eventually. I learned to surf.

A funny thing—I remember she asked me while we were out in the water what I wanted to be. Of course, I didn't have a clue and I guess I told her that. So, she asked me what I liked. And I remember—I remember telling her I liked music and feeling silly about that answer. I didn't play an instrument or sing in a choir. I didn't even own a record collection of any note. But I remember Jules telling me, "That's it then—you're going to make music."

In turn, I asked her what she wanted to be. And you know what she said? "A wife and mother." I said, "You serious?" *I mean, we were seventeen.* And she said she was serious. I should have told Tommy that—you know, later—when they were together. As his friend, I should have told Tommy and maybe he would have given her a ring sooner, before the sunglasses—before my intrusion. I'm sure it will still happen for them—they'd get married. I wanted that for Jules. She deserved to have her dream.

But it was foretelling, wasn't it? What she'd said about me and music. Because here I am and music seems to be the only thing I have to hold onto. Only I can't tell her. I can't play her my songs. Jules is not here. And neither is Tommy. And if they were, they'd surely see my songs for what they are—confessions.

ON THE BEACH ONE late morning in San Clemente, I watched the regulars doing the dance with their long boards. They gathered like seabirds, sitting their boards just beyond the surf, waiting for just the right wave. Sooner or later one of the party would drift away from the pack and I'd find myself focusing on just them—joined in our solitude, if that makes sense. On that day, I watched for close to two hours a particular guy off by himself. He'd paddle out, catch a wave, crash into the surf and do it again—rinse and repeat. He seemed determined—downright dogged in his persistence. He was, in fact, the last man on the water that morning. When he did come in, it was a few hundred yards down the beach. I watched as he tugged at his wet suit for a time then dunked his head into the surf and pulled up sweeping his dark hair back from his face—like something out of a television commercial. He tucked the board under his arm and treaded my way. As he neared, I slipped off my shades—*I just didn't want any part of that.* I sat, knees up, boots in the sand, trying not to watch him approach. But I was curious. There was something familiar about him. Had I kept my shades on, he likely would have walked right past. As it was, our eyes met. *Holy shit!*

"Hey," he said, the voice unmistakable.

"Hey," I swallowed.

He turned his soulful eyes toward the water to see what had held my attention for so long. "I never tire of it," he said, nodding at the horizon. Adjusting his grip on his board, he said, "This, on the other hand, can make an old man of me."

I just smiled. *He had to be what—thirty at the time?*

He extended his hand, "JB."

"Walk," I said.

"Mind if I sit?"

I motioned to the sand next to me.

He dropped with a long exhale. "That your bike?" he asked.

I did a head check to where I'd parked at the edge of the sand behind us. "Yep."

He nodded. "You play guitar." *It was not a question—he'd seen my case strapped to the bike.*

"I try."

He smiled. "Me too."

I laughed.

Turning the shades over and over in my hands, I tried not to stare. So mostly I just looked at his feet—*Jackson Browne's feet.*

He asked what I did and where I lived. He listened intently to my abbreviated answers. He'd heard of the dealership, but said he's never owned a car. I didn't tell him that my job there was in the past tense. We talked about L.A. for all its good and bad. He told me he preferred being away from the city and that he was staying at a friend's nearby.

"Hungry?" he asked.

"Getting there," I said.

"Come with me." He stood, brushed the sand off his backside and hoisted his board. Not questioning for even a second that I'd comply, he walked off barefoot with the board balanced on his head as I followed along pushing my bike. If the people we passed knew him, they didn't let on.

He led me to a small cedar shake house a few blocks off the beach. He propped his board against the lattice of the side porch and climbed the paint-worn steps. There he stripped his wet suit and draped it over the rail. He pushed in the unlocked screen door and turned back to me. "Bring your guitar."

The door opened into a small kitchen. Jackson was standing at the sink in a dry T-shirt and shorts. Filling a teapot, he told me to grab a seat. I leaned my guitar case against a cupboard and pulled out a chair from under the rickety aluminum table that was pushed flush under a window. On the table was a toaster.

"You drink tea?" he asked.

"Yeah. Sure."

Jackson carried two steaming, mismatched mugs to the table. "It's green tea," he told me, "—all Leah drinks."

"Leah?"

"Her place—*well*, technically her parents."

"Girlfriend?" *Idiot.*

"Something like that."

"Oh."

Jackson took his mug back to the counter where he rifled through a loaf of bread. I eyed the toaster again. He buried his head in the fridge and piled an assortment on the counter. "Sandwich sound good?"

In short order, Jackson made a pair of grilled cheese sandwiches. He sat mine on a plate in front of me and took a seat across. He then popped up and went to a cabinet above the fridge. "Secret stash," he said from a full stretch. He tossed a bag of Lays chips on the table. "Bet you can't eat just one," he joked.

Though I'd rather have had it bronzed for posterity than eat it, the sandwich was unreal—with three kinds of cheese, a slice of heirloom tomato and chopped fresh basil.

"Good huh?"

"Best."

He offered me more chips, shook a few more onto his plate then rolled up the bag and returned it to its hiding place. "Leah's got a thing about too much salt." Wiping his hands and mouth with a paper napkin, he motioned to my guitar. "You mind?"

"Sure. I mean—go ahead." I got up, took the guitar from its case and handed it to him.

"No," he said gently, "I'd like to hear you play." He leaned forward in his chair, legs crossed, elbows on knees, chin in hand, and his face no more than a few feet from mine.

"One of yours?" I offered.

He smiled. "Please—one of yours."

I played—I couldn't tell you what. I do remember his dark eyes though—so damn intense—watching mine as they darted between the frets and the floor. Never once did he look at my hands—didn't need to, I guess. The chords and my finger picking were so obvious—so second nature to him.

I kind of remember him saying—*nice*—when I'd finished. I played just the one. We went on to talk about other things as he cleaned up from lunch and we circled back to my job at the Plaza. He laughed when I told him what we called the clientele—*the Plastiques*. He joked that he was relieved to have never bought a car—much less, a Mercedes—and be spared that label. He drifted into private thought and then added with a grin that perhaps he'd used the wrong moniker for his "Pretender". I told him—no—his song is perfect as is.

Jackson yawned as the conversation started to lag.

I said, "I should get going," and I thanked him.

He rubbed his chin. "Yeah? Okay."

As the screen door bumped me on my way out, I was pretty sure I heard Jackson call, "Walk—don't be a stranger."

I WENT BY JACKSON'S place again one afternoon—took a chance he'd be there. A lady answered the door.

"Jackson here?"

"There's a chance he is. Are you, by chance, Walk?"

"Yeah," I said, "and you are Leah?"

"I am," she smiled. "Come on in, Walk."

"Great—I'm just gonna—" I leapt down the porch steps and ran to my bike for my guitar. Leah held the door smiling as I two-at-a-timed it back up the steps. She knew the drill.

"He's out back," she said as I squeezed past her.

Through the back screen door, I saw Jackson sitting cross-legged in one of twin sun-bleached director chairs. His guitar made a bridge across the wooden arms of the second chair. On his thigh, he held a yellow pad of lined paper and in his mouth the eraser end of a pencil stub. I hesitated there—the tip of my nose against the dusty screen.

"Go on," Leah said, "it's okay."

Jackson turned when he heard the door hinges complain. Seeing me, his face lit up. "Walk, you found the place. Good."

"Breadcrumbs," I said.

"Hah—good one." He picked up his guitar. "Let's head in—ya mind?—getting too hot out here."

Leah had a kettle going and three mugs on the counter. Jackson sat on the couch. I leaned my guitar against a wall and joined him there. I'd of course been there, yet the place felt unfamiliar. I guess I was a bit dumbstruck on my last visit. I looked around. The furniture was from some prior decade—colorfully patterned and well worn. Four mismatched rugs lay haphazard and overlapping on the sand-beaten hardwood. Dusty dime store figurines and tortured paperbacks cluttered a bookshelf. In the kitchen, open shelves hung in place of cabinets—chock full of food boxes and glass jars of canned vegetables. Clean and dirty dishes filled the countertop. A calico curtain hid the plumbing beneath the sink and above the fridge a lone cabinet hid Jackson's secret stash. Off the kitchen was a bedroom and I guess, a bath.

Jackson smiled when he caught me watching Leah doing stretches at the stove. She was lovely—a dancer it turned out.

We drank our tea. We talked about a lot of things—the ocean, the environment, the government, but mostly about the arts. Leah spoke excitedly about local theatre and her dance troupe. Jackson talked about recent movies, directors and actors he admired. I knew—actually met—one of the directors. He was one of Baros' clients. I kept the connection to myself figuring it'd be hard to explain. I did tell them about Jimmy and his show. It didn't ring a bell with either of them until I remembered that Jimmy went by just COLE. "Yeah-yeah," they said. They'd been in L.A. and seen the postings. "He's your friend? Well, that's cool."

It was dark before the guitars came out. I thought for a time that it wasn't going to happen.

"Mind if I start?" Jackson said. He played something new. It was gorgeous.

"Still working it out," he said.

Leah added, "He always says that—nothing's ever finished with this one." She smiled at me. "Do you have something you'd like to play for us?"

"Sure." I went for my guitar a little too eagerly and nearly tripped over Jackson's feet. I settled on a chair and readied my guitar. I made sure Jackson saw me wink at Leah. "This one's a hundred percent finished," I told her with a grin. Jackson laughed.

I started—stopped. "I call this 'Pieces of You.'" I started again and though I hadn't planned on singing, the words came out. Feeling the heat rush to my cheeks, I pressed on. On my second pass through the chorus, Jackson actually harmonized with me. I finished to them both clapping wildly and the blood rising back into my face.

We talked and played and sang into the night—trading turns and sometimes teaming up. Our tea mugs were swapped out for wine glasses and things got a little silly. Jackson tried to play slide guitar with a wine cork. When we were temporarily stumped for the next song, Leah said, "What's that song I like—come on, Jackson—you know—something like —go and call them cops, can't find good girls in a coffee shop."

"Tom Waits—'Hold On,'" I said.

Jackson smiled.

"You know it then," Leah said.

"Yeah," I said, "caught a set of his at the Troubadour a couple of months back." Jackson shook his head laughing. "Walk, you *do* get around."

We all three sang "Hold On" and called it a night.

They had me back three other times that summer and once gave me a ticket to see Jackson at the Greek. It was otherworldly, under that night sky at Griffith

Park—Jackson moving between his piano and guitar with David Lindley accompanying him on violin.

As Jackson sang about longing for Morocco and a past love—a taste of something fine, I could think only of my friends and how I wished I could've shared that night with Jules and Tommy.

## CALIFORNIA COAST/APRIL 1978

The regular crowd was packed in, asses to surfboards, at Big Sir's. Just to be clear, nobody was lugging a surfboard. Vintage longboards lined the walls as bar décor. There was not a true surfer in the place and not a one to catch the wordplay in the name.

It was open mic night, though you'd never know it beneath the beer voices. Three acts had already passed across the make-shift stage without so much as a polite clap. A folksy girl with cat-eyed glasses and a red guitar sang something popular at the time yet somehow unrecognizable. A guy duo played and sang three John Denver tunes and slunk back to their slurry girlfriends. A big lunk of a guy finger-picked a Roy Orbison song on his tiny guitar and then fumbled with the microphone to tell anyone listening, "Sorry folks, that's the only song I know."

Taps were pulled, beer was spilled, smokes were smoked. Hair was tossed, eyes batted, feels copped. Come-ons were floated, rejected, and accepted.

A young guy, early twenties, with dark eyes and long hair pulled back under a ski cap, carried his guitar overhead as he made his way to the ever-shrinking stage. He sat, brought the guitar to his knee, and tuned it unnoticed. He adjusted the height of the stand and tapped the mic once for a sound check. What came next was hard to explain. It was, as they say, a had to be there.

Just a handful nearest him took note when he began to play, listening for a familiar tune and ready to dismiss a dreaded original. It was, in fact, an original song. But the few curious didn't turn back to the din. As more ears perked to his sound, a hush spread concentrically through the bar. When he began to sing, even more turned to listen and watch.

The guys saw themselves in him, felt the pain of his loneliness, believed that they themselves had lived his words. The girls lost themselves in his eyes. They studied the lines of his face as he sang, the muscles of his forearms as he played. They saw he was half broken and thought they were the one to fix him.

When his song ended, still nobody in the place clapped. They simply waited, silently, for him to start again.

## Chapter Twenty-Three

Closing time. I sat alone at the bar drinking my payment pint. Sheila moved methodically through the place wiping surfaces and turning over chairs onto tabletops. In the smoky mirror, I'd catch her stealing glances my way as she cleaned. She was alright—early thirties—with an endearing child-like gap between her front teeth. Sheila was among a growing catalog of barmaids I'd disappoint by keeping to myself and leaving alone.

Deep in the far corner of the bar, Ned, the owner, leaned on a high-top locked in conversation with another guy his age—both fifties. When I saw the two of them approaching, I sat my beer down and turned to face them. My eyes dropped to the second man's well-worn boots and I felt a sense of relief that they weren't polished blacks.

Ned made the introductions. "Walk, I want you to meet a friend of mine. This here's Mac."

We shook. "Charlie McKenna," he said, "I caught your set tonight."

"Mac's a recorder producer. Tell him, Mac."

"Sound Engineer," he said. "Buy you a beer?"

"On the house," Ned said shuffling around the bar and setting up three Coors. He said to Mac, "Told you he could sing the phone book and still break hearts—am I right?"

Mac's reply wasn't about my music but instead about my cap. "What do you call that thing?—a beanie?"

"I don't know—a ski cap, I guess."

"That your signature, is it?"

"Nah—a gift. Easier to wear than carry I guess."

He said, "Charles Bronson wears one of those—his signature—as a tough guy."

I didn't know what I was supposed to say to that.

Ned pushed the conversation back to music. "He's pretty good on that guitar too—right?" Old Ned hung right there with us keeping the beers coming as Mac and I talked. Mac was an interesting guy with lots of stories and knowledge about the music business. He'd spent his career at Sunset Sound and worked with Joni Mitchell and The Doors, among others. He told me he lived in Laurel Canyon—said he'd built a studio in what he called "the woodshed" with scraps of equipment he'd picked up over the years.

Sheila lingered patiently long after her work was done. When Ned asked her to put on some coffee, she fired up the Mr. Coffee and went on home. After we killed a second pot, Mac asked me where I was living. I told him on the road—motels mostly. I said it suited me. He saw in my eyes that I meant it and the father in him surfaced. He offered for me to come stay with him and his wife. In that moment, it must have sounded good to me—a home. I went by the motel for my stuff and rode through the early morning hours following his Mercury into the famed Laurel Canyon in the northwest suburbs of Los Angeles. I was going home.

MAC GOT OUT OF his car on a gravel drive in front of a modest cottage house with a box-like addition jutting from its left flank. Stacked firewood ran the length of the addition—the woodshed. He waited for me at the front door. Inside, it smelled like bacon or biscuits, or both. I met his wife, Iris. She struck me as a woodland fairy who long ago traded in her wings for gray hair and arthritic hands, though it seemed to me that she kept her sprite parts.

We ate. They fixed me up in a spare room hung with the aura of a lost child's bedroom. I unpacked what little I had and fell asleep across the bed.

I woke to the sound of chopping wood and got up to find Iris in her kitchen. I was sitting with her eating a bowl of cereal when Mac came in to refill his coffee. He topped off Iris' mug and poured the rest into his thermos. "Follow me," he said.

Outside, he pushed a wheelbarrow to a wood pile at the back of the lot. He had me load it and push it back up the drive to where the splitting was done. He handed me a wedge and ten-pound sledge. "Split wood before?"

"Nope."

"Swing once to set the wedge and once to split the log." He demonstrated. "Easy as that."

"Got it."

"Stack the split wood over there against the woodshed. Keep it neat now."

After three loads, I had torn blisters on the webs of both thumbs and they were oozing a clear liquid. Mac came out to get me for lunch. He looked at my hands and then the shaft of the hammer—mangled by my ugly swings. He shook his head. "Not sure who got the worst of it. Come on and eat."

We ate. He used a roll of duct tape to wrap the splintered shaft of the hammer.

He then used the same tape to cover the blisters on my hands. I went at it for another two hours before throwing in the towel. I got a shower and we had supper together. Mac stoked the woodstove to take the chill off and we ate off our laps in front of the television.

The next day was more of the same for me—hauling, splitting, stacking. My aim with the sledge was getting better. Mid-afternoon, I noticed through a window that the lights were on in the studio. Mac came out shortly after and said, "That'll do—go get you a shower." I dressed in the clothes Iris had washed for me and with wet hair followed Mac into the studio.

"Most everything in here came from Sunset Sound," he said. "Disney built the place originally and bought only the best. The subsequent owners also didn't shy from updating things with the latest gizmos and gadgets. And they made me good deals on the old. I prefer the analog myself," he said. He put a hand atop the mixing board as if presenting a favored child. "This baby here is custom-built with UA 610 modules. And that over there is an Ampex 350—runs two-inch tape. Buffalo Springfield recorded on it. Janis Joplin too. It's a fine rig—smooth on the high end, open and bright. And those mics there—Neumann's—none better."

It was great and all, but I couldn't help but wonder what he built it for. After my tour, he simply turned off the lights and locked the door.

It must have been late June, which meant I'd been with the McKenna's for over a month. They didn't ask much of me other than the log splitting and to join them for their evening meal. I don't mean it to sound like we didn't bond because we did. It's just that they had their routines and I pretty much kept to myself.

Iris would work mornings at the local school cafeteria, so she'd be gone before dawn and come home shortly after lunch. Mac got up with her, backed his Chevy truck up to the woodpile, and had the truck loaded by daybreak. He'd have his coffee and fried eggs for breakfast and retreat to his studio until Iris returned. They'd have a late lunch together, sometimes out on the porch where they'd watch me split and stack. On occasion, they'd ask me to join them, but I'd decline. After lunch, Iris would piddle in her garden. Mac would leave in his truck and not come back until evening with the truck bed emptied. I offered a few times to go with him—help unload—but he said he enjoyed the alone time. Iris would joke that he had a girlfriend. Mac would counter with, "What makes you think it's just one?" Like I said—a routine.

After supper was their evening walk. I'd stay back and clean up the dishes. Before bed, it was the eleven o'clock news followed by Carson. Iris was a sucker for a pun and loved Johnny's Carnac. Mac recounted the time when the divine visitor from the east held the sealed envelope to his headdress and said, *Mount Baldy*, to the question—*What did Yul Brynner's wife do on their wedding night?* Mac said Iris laughed so hard she peed her pants. She didn't deny it. She did say that she liked it even better when the joke bombed and Carnac would bestow a curse on the audience—*May a diseased yak befriend your sister.* Mac said that Iris liked that particular curse because she didn't get on with his sister, Barb. "I've got no beef with that woman," Iris said. Mac gave me a wink and circled back to tell me that Mount Baldy is actually the local's nickname for nearby Mount San Antonio—the highest point in Los Angeles County.

I do believe they liked having me around—we felt like family. Far as I could tell by the photos around the house, they had a daughter—once. But they didn't talk about her.

MOST DAYS, I'D SPLIT wood 'till one or two o'clock. While Mac was gone in the afternoons, I'd write—but not at the house. I'd strap my guitar to my bike and explore Laurel Canyon—riding until I'd find a spot where the sun attached itself to a tree, a rock, a signpost, or a sleeping dog. I sometimes wished to be that mindless object or dog—bathed in the sun's warmth and free of thought. Free of the memories of all that happened to me since the day Alistair Whittacker came to the Plaza. Try as I might, I could not rectify the things I'd done. Writing a song was the only way to relieve that burden. When the words and melodies eluded me, I'd shut off my bike and coast—winding all the way down to the bottom of the hill and the Canyon Store. Sometimes, I'd get a sandwich or a piece of fruit inside but always I'd sit in a rocker on the store porch to watch the comings and goings—watching the sun going down and the world spinning 'round.

One afternoon, I came back up the hill to find Iris tending her garden. I toted a heavy pale of clippings for her and dumped it on the compost pile.

"Can I ask you something?" I said.

"Shoot."

"It's about Mac."

"Well now, about him I can't promise a sensible answer."

I said, "He brought me here because he liked my music."

"I think that's fair to say—among other reasons."

"And he's got that studio in there—that just sits empty."

Iris plucked a cluster of string beans and dropped them into her up-turned apron. "Go on."

"Why do you think he hasn't asked me in there to record anything?"

"Well now, that's complicated."

"How so?"

"Put yourself in his shoes. He likes your music, yes. But he also likes you. He cares for you. He's shared his home with you."

"I'm grateful," I said.

"And it shows. But we know so little about you. Mac respects your privacy. The only thing he's sure of about you is that you're hiding—from someone or something. Would he be right in either assumption?"

"Both."

"Fair enough," she said. "Now suppose he helps you record those songs of yours. Then what? Do you circulate them? Do you put your name out there?"

"I see what you mean."

Iris stooped to resume her hunt among the bush beans. "—or else."

"Or else what?"

"Or else he's just waiting for you to ask him."

I looked across the yard at the woodshed. "Do you think we could maybe make some demos and then decide?"

"That's between you and him." Iris straightened up and leaned way back at the waist to stretch. "So ask him already."

That same afternoon, Iris asked me to accompany her down the mountain to pick up groceries. Said she wanted to give me a chance to pick out some things that I liked to eat. She drove that Mercury like a bat out of hell—her elfin size making it impossible to both reach the brakes and see over the dashboard at the same time.

I asked the stock clerk if they had Eggo waffles. He said they didn't. I picked up a banana bunch and a bag of Oreos so Iris could feel like she was treating me.

Leaving the store with our fortifications, Iris chuckled. She stood square on the grocer's porch and cackled. "A sight I'll not soon forget—standing right over there wearing the Queen's red cape."

"A cape? Who?"

"Crosby," she said, "that nut-ball."

"Crosby? David Crosby?"

"That'd be the one—prancing around like a deranged rooster."

"Really? No kidding?"

"Now that other one, that friend of his—Nash. Now he was sure a handsome fellow."

I stood there imagining the scene.

"Come along now," she called over her shoulder—like a hen to her chick.

Iris roasted chicken that night—Mac's favorite—to soften him up. At the table, I didn't know how to ask him so I passed the potatoes and let it rip. "Mac, you think we could maybe record some of my songs?"

Mac plopped a heaping spoonful of mashed potatoes on his plate, looked up at me, and said simply, "Suppose so."

MAC TOOK WHAT SEEMED like forever setting up while I paced in the wings. By the time he said,

"Wait for my hand signal to start and give me three seconds of quiet when you finish," I had to pee so bad. But I didn't want to delay things any further, so I took my seat. I asked, "What do you want me to play?"

"Give me what you played back at Ned's."

I nervously strummed a few chords and started to sing. He stopped me. "Just the guitar part—we'll do vocals later."

I had a hard time keeping my place in the song without singing. And I kept messing up the tempo. It was a rocky start to say the least. But Mac didn't seem bothered. He'd listen through headphones and nod along—not smiling but not grimacing either. After each take, he'd adjust things—add a mic, take one away, move it one inch in one direction or another. I was emotionally exhausted after the first song and was ready to burst. Thankfully, Iris ignored the flashing RE-CORDING light outside the door and walked right in with a pitcher of sun tea and some glasses. Mac was pissed but I could have kissed her. I ran to pee. We only did one more song that first day—and we redid them both the next. We spent fifteen days in the woodshed recording five songs. Then, suddenly, I was on the outside looking in. Mac booted me, making it clear that he, and he alone, did the mixing. All that creative outpouring and then nothing. I was going crazy. I killed one day putting new brakes on the Mercury, but then went right back to pacing around outside the studio. Having had enough, Iris finally stuck her head out the kitchen window and yelled "STOP—just stop." She said, "You're gonna piss him off and it's me that's gotta live with him."

At dinner almost two weeks later, Mac presented me a cassette tape. I'll never forget the feeling of holding that tape and reading the hand-written label with my name on it. The three of us rushed off to the studio and left our meals to go cold on the table.

My songs sounded good—great even—so much better than I expected. It was me—sure—but enhanced in ways that only Mac could have pulled off. The layering, the overdubs, all of it—so amazing. Mac made no bones about what he thought of the songs. He hooted and stomped and kept calling them "canned magic" as we played through them. Iris angrily hushed him but then joined in herself, shaking her head and saying again and again, "I don't believe it! I really-really don't believe it."

## THE DAKOTA/NEW YORK CITY/FEBRUARY 1970

"You didn't need the magic, John. It was already in you. Always in you." "John?"

"But I sampled the magic all the same, didn't I."

"Yes, John, but not like him."

"He took proper advantage of his turns; I'll say that much."

"He did."

"Pinched his 'Yesterday' in a dream. Said as much. Marched it around, *'Have you heard this one, boys? Woke up with it, I did.'* Scrambled Eggs he called it. Bloody brilliant we told him. You're a bloody genius, Paul."

"That's Paul. But you're two different people. You are stronger on your own. You're on your own now, John."

"You don't say? On my own? What are you then? Because it's never just me. It's always us. John and Yoko. That's what they're saying. John and Yoko."

"Am I in your head, John?"

"My head? The truth? You and every bloody one else."

"Do you need a break, John?"

"A break, is it? I need a good scream—a good, long, loud fucking scream."

"Tell me, John. Really. Tell me what it is you need."

"Need? Fucking need? I need Julia—I need my mum. Alright? I need Stu. I need my Uncle George. Can you do that, Yoko? Can you bring back my dead mum?"

"Do you need me, John?"

"—the fuck do I know what I need. I need the sunglasses. The fuck do I know."

John Lennon left Yoko and New York, heading west to Los Angeles for what was later called his Lost Weekend. Yoko packed him off with their assistant, Mai Pang, with instructions for her to give John what he needed—anything he needed. They rented out Peter Lawford's house, formally the Louis B. Mayer estate in Santa Monica. The 'Weekend' and the affair lasted eight months. It was a creative rebirth for John resulting in the album, *IMAGINE*.

## Chapter Twenty-Four

I CAME IN FROM splitting wood and filled a glass under the sink faucet. I drank it down in one long pull and filled it again. Sweat ran from my forehead into my eyes, down my temples, and into my newly grown beard.

I spun the paper towel roll and tore off a three-sheeter. I wiped at my brow and neck, lifting sweat and sawdust both. Wadding up the ball of wet pulp, I eyed the trash can and took my shot—*a rare miss.*

Bending to retrieve my miss from behind the can, I saw a yellow scrap of paper and scooped them both up together. I reformed the soggy ball, backed away and fired again—*nothing but net.*

I began to ball up the yellow scrap when I noticed something written on it. Curious, I unfolded it. It was a phone message—a name and number. I read the name—*Allison.* No, that wasn't right.

I flattened the note, read it again. *Alistair.*

I CAME LATE TO the table. Iris and Mac were already seated and waiting. When he saw me, Mac took up his fork and went to stab a pork chop from the platter. Before he could, I placed the yellow note dead-center on his plate. He looked down at the note and let go of the fork. He pushed back from the table, removed the napkin from his lap and dropped it over his plate and the note.

"I suppose the name means something to you?" he said.

When I didn't answer, he stood and turned away from the table. Eyes to the floor, he rung his hands. "He's a musician and a friend," he said. Mac looked toward Iris. "—spent some time with us—in hiding." He looked at me. "My guess is you already know why." He went to the window and looked out into the yard, fiddling with the shade. "We hadn't heard from him in over a year then—out of the blue—he called asking for a favor." Mac swallowed. "He told me where I might find you."

I looked at Iris who was holding onto the edge of the table like a lifeline. I saw the tension in her when she spilled, "He just wanted you to be checked on—to make sure you were alright." She looked at Mac. "That's the truth," he said. "Alistair was worried about you but wouldn't say why. I did as he asked. I called around the area he thought you might be—checked with some friends. And sure enough, Ned told me he knew of a kid that fit the description."

Mac came around and stood in front of me. "And here you are." He reached out to lay a hand on my shoulder, but I pulled away. He sat back down, lifted the napkin off his plate, and cleared his throat. "We should eat."

My duffle and guitar by my side, I sat on the front porch step—hungry, undecided.

The screen door opened and Mac came up behind me. "I'll tell you what I know, but it ain't much."

I didn't flinch.

"You wanna hear it or not?"

I nodded.

"Alistair played cello—no—that's an understatement—he's a maestro—London Symphony, the whole nine yards."

Realizing he'd left out what he thought to be an important note, Mac said, "Alistair's British." He went on. "We met at Sunset Sound. I was working late one night and heard a banging on the door. This was back in what—'75. Anyway, I opened the door and here's this tall fellow with striking eyes standing in the rain holding a cello case. He said he was looking for work—as a studio musician. I brought him into the studio and we got to talking. Before our talk ended, I'd invited him to stay with us."

I looked over at Mac who was now seated next to me.

"Yeah," he said, "—followed me home just like you. Stayed with us that summer—maybe four months. He was a good guest—very polite—in that British sort of way. In those four months, he never really talked about himself. Until one night, near about the time he left us, I convinced him to help me polish off a fifth of Black label." Mac laughed, "Alistair was no drinking man. So that night, he opened up a bit. Told me he played for the Beatles. Said he knew them all but was closest to George. He went on to share some stories about the band. He told me it was ugly at the end—a real shame. Then, quick as it started, he stopped talking. I dunno, but it sure seemed to me that there was much more he didn't say. But I saw no cause to press it. Things were clear enough. He was carrying some deep dark secret—dark enough to keep him on the run."

Mac stood and stretched, looking embarrassed it seemed to me. He said, "Alistair left us a package. I didn't open it until after he was gone. It was money—a fair amount of it. Enough that we—Iris and me—wouldn't have to worry."

I looked out to the stack of firewood thirty feet long. "The wood—you don't sell it, do you?"

"Nope—give it away—to friends mostly, and others who look like they could use it."

"Robin Hood."

'Something like that."

I asked, "So you heard from him again? When he told you about me?"

"That's right. He asked for my help. I figured I owed him, you know, because of—" Mac looked hard at me, "Walk—"

"Yeah?"

"There was something else in the package—besides the money."

"What?"

Mac told me it was an album—one of John's—a solo effort.

"Which one?"

"*Walls and Bridges*—released late the prior year, 1974. You know it?"

"Not really," I said.

"He left a note with it." Mac handed it to me.

The note read—*Mac, #9 his confession. More I cannot say. AW*

"What does it mean?"

"Was hoping you might—"

"Do you have the record?"

In the studio, Mac handed me the album. On the cover was John Lennon wearing five pairs of glasses in varied styles. I thought—four Beatles plus one. *The sunglasses*. In the liner notes, I pointed to the song "#9 Dream".

"Yeah," Mac said, "—listened to it many times and still don't know what Alistair, or John, were trying to say. Mean anything to you?"

"I know that John was obsessed with the number—his birthdate, first home address, Beatles first gig at the Cavern Club, and first appearance on Ed Sullivan both on February 9th."

"So—you know your Beatles. They play a role in it—don't they?"

I handed the record back to Mac. "Let's listen."

When the song's long refrain ended, Mac grabbed a fistful of his sandy hair pulling it straight up from his receding hairline. "Gibberish," he said, "Drug-induced nonsense. *Ah! Bowakawa, poussé, poussé*. What is that?"

I didn't have a clue about the meaning of the refrain, but the lyrics were a different matter entirely.

*So long ago, was it in a dream, was it just a dream?*
*I know, yes, I know, it seemed so very real to me*
*Somebody calling out my name—John, as it started to rain,*
*two spirits dancing so strange*
*Dream, dream away, magic in the air, was magic in the air?*
*believe, yes, I believe, more I cannot say, what more can I say?*

"John couldn't have described it better," I said.

"Described what?"

"It's like Alistair said in his note—it's John's confession. And like John says in his song—*more I cannot say.*"

"And you?" Mac asked, "—can you say more?"

"I'd be guessing," I lied. "Mac," I said, "in your professional opinion—looking at their body of work—do you believe there was magic involved with the Beatles?"

He plowed the lines in his forehead with his thumbs. "Figuratively?—no question about it. They were a once in a lifetime—once in a century even. Literally?—I don't know—you tell me." Mac fell deep into thought. He smiled to himself.

"What?" I asked.

"Annie," he said, "our girl—she was little then. I remember us talking about the Beatles and—what was it she said?—*They have so many good songs... it's like they're hogging them.*"

"Sweet," I said, "and she's got a point."

I looked Mac in the eyes. "I assume Alistair's phone number is no good."

"Yup. It's a different number every time," Mac confirmed.

I said, "If he calls again, I want to talk to him."

About their Annie—they told me her story—abusive boyfriends, drugs, free love, found Jesus and a new *family*. Iris said it simply, "The '60s took her."

"*Ninety-six, ninety-seven, ninety-eight, ninety-nine, one hundred.*" I flipped over to my back and started on my crunches—*one, two, three, four.* I heard three quick taps on my door.

"Walk—you decent?" It was Iris.

"*Fifteen, sixteen, seventeen,* yep—come in."

She pushed in the door. "You planning on finishing anytime soon?"

"—*Twenty-nine, thirty, thirty-one*—yeah, what's up?"

"There's a Mr. Browne on the phone for you—*Jackson* Browne."

I lifted the phone from the counter, "Jackson!"

"Yeah, Walk. How you doing?"

I could hear the smile in his voice. I was smiling myself. "I'm good—yeah—all good here."

"You're out of breath. Did I interrupt something?"

"Uh—no—just—did you get my tapes?"

"I did—yeah—listen—that's why I'm calling."

"So you got 'em—Best!"

"Walk—listen—what are you doing next Saturday? *What is that? What? The 17th?* Yeah, what are you doing Saturday the 17th?"

"Uh—not sure—I mean, nothing I guess—I'm not doing anything."

"*Good*—good. Take this down. Civic Auditorium, Portland, Oregon, Saturday, August 17th. Got that?"

"Yeah—sure—got it. You playing there?"

"I was—yeah—but now *you* are."

"Huh?"

"Yeah, see. I promised a show to the Sierra Club. You know them?"

"Uh, yeah, I think so."

"Yeah? Okay good. They do good work—for the environment. But see—there was a mix-up. I'm double booked. So I talked to them—told them about you. And they agreed—you know—since the tickets are sold and all. I promised them another date next Spring. So—what do you think?"

"What do I think?"

"Yeah, about playing for me—in my place—in Portland."

"I'm not sure—I mean—"

"Listen, Walk, I've heard your tapes. Your stuff is great. You're ready—and you'd be doing me a huge favor. Now there's no back-up band. I was doing it solo—just me and my piano. So it would be just you—you know—solo acoustic."

Jackson said more but I didn't catch it all. He thanked me again and said his goodbye. I aimlessly laid the phone back on the counter as I realized—*Jackson must of booked me using my real name, not Bucko as I'd been using.*

Iris put the phone back on the receiver. She took a seat at the table and patted a hand on the empty chair next to her, smiling. "News?" she asked.

*I was going to Portland—via Los Angeles.*

## ABC STUDIOS/NEW YORK CITY/OCTOBER 1974

COSELL: "This is Howard Cosell, the name of the show is Speaking of Everything, my guest is Mr. John Lennon, one of the Beatles. You remember the Beatles, who brought a whole new form of musical culture to the United States of America in the early sixties when they debuted on the then existent variety show known as The Ed Sullivan Show. There have been many vicissitudes in the lives of the four respective Beatles and perhaps none more notable than in the case of our guest, Mr. John Lennon, who's had a wide variety of troubles and yet continuing artistic successes. All of which we shall begin to discuss with you. It's a joy to have you with us."

LENNON: "Thank you, Howard. It's a pleasure to be here and it's great to meet you—seeing you on TV so much."

COSELL: "It's a treasured moment for you—"

LENNON: "It is—one of the highlights."

Laughter

COSELL: "John, let us get right to the heart of your troubles and get those out of the way—the continuing and apparent attempt by the United States and its government to effectuate your deportation from this country..."

LENNON: "So my case is still up in the air and once a year, they tell me I have thirty days to get out. It seems to have started by a Senator Thurmbold or somebody—"

COSELL: "Strom Thurman."

LENNON: "Yeah, that's the one. It sounded like something that happens to you in old age. I got a stromthurman in my arm."

Laughter

COSELL: "That was going to be my next question. I've read on several occasions that 'This time, Lennon has got to go' and yet it is not eventuated..." "I just wanted to spend another minute or two on your case and then get to—to your music, your career, the career of your former colleagues, and some respects still. You had wanted the man who originally prosecuted you, plus the chief immigration officer, in a more contemporary proceeding..."

LENNON: "The point was when it started, the immigration people were adamant it was their own local decision and there was nothing to be done—a technicality—it was the law. And all the time we disclaimed that and said, no, we think the instructions were coming from Washington..." "And it turned out subsequently that we were right. But now—we can't—they won't let us get at the people who would be honest about it."

―――――――――

Source: Excerpts from *LIVE ABC* radio transcript—October 6, 1974

## Chapter Twenty-Five

Back in L.A. for the first time since I'd disappeared—the night Kim was killed and I deserted Tommy when he needed me most—I moved through the city like a ghost. I had so many personal demons in that angel town.

I pulled from my wallet the number I'd swiped from my mom's address book and called my dad from a phone booth. To hear his voice again, after so long, was strange. I wasn't sure how'd it go, but we got through it with only a few awkward moments. Of course I did most of the talking. He did say he was having a hard time seeing me with a guitar. "*You were always listening to music but never once playing.*" I told him it was a recent development. He said he'd heard about me working on cars. "*One day you're a mechanic and the next you're playing guitar in front of people.*" He one hundred percent thought I was kidding him when I told him about the concert near him in Oregon. I even left out the part about it being at Jackson Browne's request. He seemed sincere about coming—took down the date and address. I told him I'd leave a ticket for him at will call. I asked him if he needed two. He said, no, that it was just him. He thanked me for calling and my dad hung up.

He never once asked about my mom.

I made the climb to the Hollywood sign—back to where my life began—the part that mattered anyway—the part with Tommy and Jules.

It was early morning of the day I was going to see Jimmy. Placing the palm of my hand on the D—still cold and untouched by the rising sun—I felt the familiar sting of adolescence played out in the halls of Hollywood High; my acne, the cliques, me mad as hell at Tommy for lying—playing me for the fool—fucking up my mid-terms.

And then, her face—Jules' face. Jules on top of me grabbing at my flailing fists—me yelling at her to *get off*—and everything changed. The joint—her warm can of Coke—floating from her lips to mine. Her soft hands on mine, saying let go—*leggo*. The broken bottle of syrup—the way we laughed. The toast—warm and buttery—the three of us in that stranger's kitchen. Tommy taking Jules home on my bike. Me waiting—alone again. But he came back—Tommy came back. We were friends. *Best.*

BACK ON THE STREETS, I dialed the number I knew by heart. I tapped nervously as it rang.

"Good afternoon, Plaza Motors, Kimberly speaking."

I hesitated. "Excuse me, did you say your name was Kimberly?"

"Yes, sir, I did."

"And this is Plaza Motors—on Santa Monica?"

"Correct, sir. Can I help you in some way?"

"It's just that—I knew another Kim—she worked there—at the desk—like you."

"I wouldn't know about that, sir, I've only been here for a short time."

"But it's strange though, right? Two receptionists—both named Kim."

"Actually, my name's Kimberly. I don't go by Kim."

"She—oh—sure—sorry."

Silence.

"How can I help you, sir?"

"Oh—right. I'd like to talk to your Service Manager, Tommy—Tommy Scanlon."

"Mr. Scanlon is our Sales Manager. Is that who you were wanting, or would you like to be transferred to Parts and Service?"

"No—I mean—yes—I'd like to speak with Tommy."

"Mr. Scanlon is with a customer at present. Can I give him a message?"

"Uh-yeah. Tell him Walk called and that I'll try him back later."

"Is that a first or last name, sir?"

"Neither—it's a—you know what—just skip it. I'll try him later."

"As you wish, sir." Kimberly #2 hung up.

SEATED ON THE BUS, I watched him board at the next stop. Out the window to my left was the Plaza—my nostalgia bittersweet. My fingers clutched at my shirt for the name patch that wasn't there.

He ambled down the bus aisle—eyes down—Jimmy style. As he neared, I stuck a leg out. "I believe this seat has your name on it." I smiled up at him and slid over. Jimmy was shocked—overjoyed. He stood there, his trusty can opener and fork bulging from his worn front pocket. The bus lurched forward, sending him sprawling down on top of me.

"Walk!" he said excitedly.

"Cole," I said coolly, eyes forward.

He put his hand on my shoulder, squeezed. "I can't believe it."

"Believe it," I said.

"Where you been?"

"Later," I said in a hushed voice.

His head swiveled. "Okay—yeah," he whispered. Jimmy looked me over good. Smiling, he rubbed his jaw.

"Yeah," I said, "beard's new. What's new with you?—still painting?"

"Every day," he said.

"And Esse?"

"Doing good—yeah, she doing all right."

I wanted to ask about Melissa but didn't. Tommy and Jules would come later.

"Walk," he said, disbelieving, "you disappeared."

"Next stop's ours," I said.

Jimmy looked out, "Chinatown?"

"Yep. Wah's sound good?"

OVER BOWLS OF STEAMING rice and a shared plate of pork dumplings, we spoke freely among the English-challenged staff. I told Jimmy about my time on the road, meeting Jackson, my songwriting, and my upcoming show in Portland. Jimmy said, "See now—ain't fair—you got the lunchbox and the talent."

Jimmy told me what the papers said about Kim's death—that it was a murder suicide—that Kim shot him. Made sense, I guess. Staging Peter as the victim would draw scrutiny to her as the crazed girlfriend and leave Peter's past buried. Kim's death hurt me all over again. Jimmy never asked what made me leave so abruptly—but he had to wonder about the coincidence of being on the same night of Kim's death.

I had to prod him to talk about his painting. He said that Melissa still represented him with a permanent residency at her gallery as well as getting his work placed at galleries in Chicago, New York, and coming soon, Amsterdam. I teased him about being world renowned. He and Esse still lived at the same apartment on Grape—said she'd never leave. He told me he'd rented the empty apartment next door and set Essie up with a new recliner, a nice rug, and a television. She sat in there for one day and came right back—said she missed the smell of his paints.

Esse went right back to her hard chair in the kitchen.

I asked Jimmy about Tommy, opening with the news that I heard he made Sales Manager. "Yeah," Jimmy said, "business is good. I can hardly keep up anymore."

"So you're staying," I said.

"Yeah," he said, "funny thing, Walk. Painting just don't feel like a job to me—and who knows how long it will last. Working at the Plaza—that's real. Besides, I look around and think—who am I to be throwing away a perfectly good job."

"Tommy," I said, circling back, "—he doing okay?"

"Yeah—sure seem so—he's getting married."

"You're kidding?—with Jules—when?"

"Kimberly. His fiancée's name is Kimberly."

"Kimberly?" I sputtered.

"You don't know her. She's our receptionist—at the Plaza—she's new."

"But—where's Jules—Julia Nichols?"

"She's gone—been gone."

My heart seized. "Since when?"

"Since it all—you, Kim—*it all*."

"Where is she?"

"Don't know for sure. Think I heard maybe back east?"

Jimmy excused himself to go use the can. I sat hunched in my seat with the wind knocked out of me. Jules was on the east coast—likely in Boston with her sister Trudy and Kurt. Jules was gone—from Tommy, from L.A., from me. Jules was in Boston—among those east coast men with their pedigrees and diplomas, their accents and their charms. All this time away on the road, I held it together because I thought I was doing right by Jules and Tommy. I pictured them together—and happy—free of me and my intrusion.

When Jimmy came back, I told him I had a plane to catch. "Right. Portland," he said. "You're gonna kill it, Walk."

Outside, we held each other—long enough to say everything else we needed to say. *Goodbye, good friend. Goodbye.*

I left Jimmy there on the streets of Chinatown and disappeared once again, this time into a sidewalk flurry the colors of confetti. I jumped a westbound bus to the gray airport hotel where the bellman held my guitar and duffle. I slipped him a five and boarded the shuttle to LAX.

"Welcome aboard." The attendant stood outside the cabin door with her perfectly plastic hair and perfectly pretend smile. I handed her my ticket. Without taking it, she gave it a glance. "You'll keep that," she said, "32B—past the wing, window seat on your left. Enjoy your flight."

Stopping at row 32, I doubled-checked my ticket. I opened the overhead cabinet and stowed my duffle. I stood over the man in the aisle seat. He looked up, sighed, and undid his seatbelt. He squeezed into the aisle. I side-stepped him and took my seat. He sat down with a thud and buckled in for the second time. As I buckled, he looked my way and I nodded. From the small window, I watched men in jumpsuits load the belly of the plane. I watched for my guitar case but didn't see it. The guy beside me appeared to doze off. I looked at his shoes. He wore dress blacks—size thirteens it looked like. His soles were worn and the shoes didn't appear to have been polished since they left the box. He wasn't one of them. I counted three other pairs of spit-shined dress blacks on the way to my seat. About those I couldn't be sure.

TAKE-OFF. Being flung into the sky felt right to me—the fierceness of it matched my disposition. Three thousand feet above and still my earthly guilt suffocated me. I'd been given a gift—the power to see through another's eyes, know their mind, share their talents. Yet I chose to use the magic for selfish reasons. I've told you my story—the one where Kim's dead and Jules is gone. Jules is gone and she's not loving Tommy and she's certainly not loving me. At least I got to help Jimmy show the world his art. And I cleared Peyton's name, though too late for him. I'd decided, up there among the clouds, that my time with the sunglasses would end. I'd return them to their rightful owner—and not to those who'd kill to get them back. Peter's files went back as far as JFK. I want to believe that Jack used the sunglasses for good—to make the world a better, safer place. But their power and the power of the people behind them wrought only darkness and tragedy for the Kennedy's, didn't it? How the sunglasses fell into the hands of the Beatles I don't know. But it's pretty clear that John and Paul used them to give the world beautiful music and their friendship may have paid the price. Hoping to mend the band, I'm guessing George gave them to Whittacker who went into hiding for years, reemerging that September day at the dealership. Did Whittacker leave them behind intentionally or was it a mistake? Either way, it was fate that led me here.

## MOTEL VASHON/PORTLAND/SEPTEMBER 1978

He finished on top of her. Her face turned away. Her thighs pinned painfully under his knees. His thick hands throttling her. He pushed off her, brusque and bruising.

He doesn't frequent hookers. He's treated himself. It's what he does on kill days.

She'll remember the pain and humiliation, but not the face. He has that kind of face. Unremarkable. It served him well in his line of work. For him, the wait had been too long, for a kill day and a hooker. He got hard when he took the call from his old buddy, Brandt.

Portland's not exactly a hotbed of covert activity for the Brotherhood. There's not much need for kills here and he hates the city for it. But then he hates most everything; his ex, his boss from his day job, his Marine sergeant, the officers that oversaw his court martial, the Vietnamese woman and her young daughter that he butchered.

But never mind all that, today's a good day. He's got himself a new mark. He'll face him first, before he does the deed, that's his trademark. He fancies himself as the autograph collector.

He was dressed now and sat heavy on the edge of the bed to tie his shoes. He stopped to use the corner of the bed sheet to polish their black to a killer shine.

He grinned to himself thinking, today he'd get his autograph and his kill.

But in two days' time, he'd be dead, stabbed in the neck by a random homeless woman after he callously kicked aside her sidewalk menagerie.

CLIMBING FROM THE TAXI with duffle and guitar in hand, I looked up at the building before me—Civic Auditorium, 222 SW Clay Street, Portland, Oregon.

Inside, I asked for a Carly Helm. I was directed to her office at the back of the building. I stood out of sight in her doorway for a time watching her—busy behind her makeshift desk—unsure whether this young lady was in fact the stage manager. She was decidedly not a California girl. Her skin was winter white—nothing like the bronzed girls from home. Her hair was blond—but unnaturally so. It was platinum—and pretty. Her eyes appeared both green and brown. Hazel—best I could tell. And her lashes were long and dark, enhanced with mascara in a striking way. She wore a flannel shirt—checked red and black. She wore it open at the collar where a spray of fine moles ran along her collarbone. Her sleeves were rolled up, exposing the delicate bones of her slender wrists. All of it and the girl herself seemed a mystery to be solved. I could only smile when she looked up and caught me in my watchful act. Her eyes sparkled as they met mine then trailed down to my guitar case. She rose from her chair, hand extended. "You must be our talent. Carly," she said.

I took her hand and held it. "Walk—Jeff Walker."

"So glad you're here, Walk-Jeff-Walker."

"Just Walk," I said.

"You come to us all the way from sunny L.A. on the recommendation of *the* Jackson Browne. You, Walk-Jeff-Walker, are most certainly not *just* anybody."

I smiled.

"You can let go of my hand now."

"Oh—sorry." I let go of her and dropped my hand to my side.

She took a sheet of paper from her desk. "We have a room for you at the Concord—not two blocks away." She opened a drawer and pulled out a key for me. "I took the liberty of pre-checking you in. Would you like to go there now, or do you want a tour of the place?"

"The tour—I guess."

"Sure. Great. Just give me a minute and I'll show you around."

I stood there.

"I'll be out in the hall in just a minute," she smiled. "I promise."

I was looking through the glass of a display case when Carly came up behind me and touched my sleeve. In her nearness, I felt something entirely new to me—a warm calm inside. I felt fixed somehow.

"We're formally the Keller Theater," she said, "—name was changed to Civic Auditorium in 1966."

I pointed to a framed photograph. "JFK was here."

"That's right. Senator Jack Kennedy spoke at the Keller on September 7, 1960. He'd be elected president in a year and shot dead in three more." She stood, wistful in the moment, then moved down the glass case waving for me to follow. "Here's one that might interest you more. Led Zeppelin played a packed house here on December 29, 1968."

"That must have been something," I said.

"I was eleven years old—but, yeah, I'm sure it was."

"So that makes you—"

"Twenty-one. Thanks for asking."

"Twenty-one and in charge of this place."

"Not in charge—Stage Manager—and this place isn't what it used to be. Today, we book mostly local."

"Yeah, but still—"

"There's no *still*. Our headliner last weekend was a band called Seafood Mama."

"I see your point. But hey, Jackson Browne—"

"What's that they say? Close only counts in horseshoes and hand grenades. You're here. He's not. No offense."

"None taken."

"Want to see our stage?"

"Lead the way, my Queen."

"Don't get cute."

"There's no cute. Nobody's cute here. I mean, you're cute—"

"Are you quite finished?"

"Looks that way. Yup—finished."

REHEARSAL WENT FINE—just me, the sound guy, and the lighting guy. It felt silly really. I clunked through two songs and called it. I was hoping maybe Carly would sit through it, but I guess she had better things to do. I couldn't find her after either, so I asked directions and made my way to the hotel and my room.

ROUNDING THE CORNER at 3rd Street, some guy must have noticed my guitar and asked for my autograph. *My autograph?* I thought it was a stretch—even told him so, but he looked like a tourist and seemed genuinely appreciative. He pulled out a pen and I signed for him the program Carly had given me. He stood eerily still and read my name back to me—*Jeff Walker*. There was something off about him—but I managed a smile and said back to him, "That's right." As he turned to walk away, I noticed his shoes.

THE HOTEL WAS OLD and creaky like stepping back into a dreamy black and white movie. At the front desk, a nice lady helped me box a package for the outgoing mail. It was something I'd given a lot of thought, and it was time. She didn't flinch at the address— *John Lennon, The Dakota, New York, New York.*

In my room, I laid across the high bed. There, I slept—dreamed—no longer golden, but frenzied and red.

I woke in the dark. My clothes were soaked through with stress sweat. There was a note slipped under the door. It was from Carly.

*Walk—Jeff—Walker,*
*Come by 7. You're ON at 7:30.*
*Took care of your ticket request.*
*Break a leg!*
*Queen Carly*

I checked my watch. *Shit!* I was late.

RUNNING FULL SPRINT DOWN the sidewalk, I realized I didn't know the way into backstage. I rushed in through the lobby and saw no choice but to wade through the people filling the aisles and milling around their seats. *Damn*—all these people! *Did they not get the word that Jackson wasn't coming?* I maneuvered down a side aisle and climbed the stairs to stage left. I intended to slip backstage and *what?*—was I to be introduced? *I had no idea.* I unlatched my guitar case and strapped on my Gibson. And I stood—off to the left of the stage—unsure, unmoving.

I peered across the stage and saw Carly step out just beyond the curtain. She gave a discreet hand signal to Owen the lighting guy and the house lights dimmed. As if on command, the crowd took their seats and the noise level dropped from deafening to dead. I fixed my eyes on Carly. I saw her lips part as she mouthed—*are you okay?* I shook my head in a manner that was no answer at all. Carly smiled. She smiled at me and with both arms made a gentle sweeping motion encouraging me to step forward and take the stage.

I felt my legs moving beneath me and heard myself croak into the microphone.
"Good evening, everybody."
*Nothing. Some stirring in seats.*
"As you can see, I'm obviously not Jackson Browne."
*More silent stirring.*
"—Jackson is much taller and a lot better looking."
*A few clapped.*

"—He told me to say that."

*More clapped, some laughed, and I finally took my first breath.*

I went on. "I'm Jeff Walker—people call me Walk." I said, "Jackson was very sure I was ready for this. But standing here on this stage, alone, looking out at so many of you—I'm just not sure what he was thinking."

*A few unsure claps.*

"He said to me—he said—Walk, you won't be alone. I sent my piano. And to his credit, he did. There it is—his baby." I pointed to his grand piano as if it wasn't already obvious to them. "Well, I don't play piano."

*A few unsure claps and a moan or two.*

"But here we are and I don't suppose you'd forgive me—or Jackson—if I'd, right now, up and run off this stage. So if it'd be alright with you I'd like to start off with one of Jackson's songs—'Late for the Sky.'"

For the first time that night—*applause*. I clung to my guitar for dear life and I played and I sang Jackson's song about being awake again—no longer able to pretend. A song about trying to understand how my life had led me here— alone again and late for the sky.

IT WAS NOT UNLIKE the golden slumbers—on that stage yet outside of my body. In a place—*the mystic*—where not everyone can go. Only the lucky ones, I suppose. And yet, I'd gladly trade that moment to get back home—to the warmth of their smiles, their voices, their laughter—back to the smells of that toaster and to once again taste the sweet salty butter on my tongue.

Once there was a way to get back home—but that path had been torched. So I went back the only way I could—through my songs—and I took the audience along with me.

When my story had played out—after I'd sung all the songs I had to sing—I left the stage. I exited the mystic and crashed back down to my life as it was, suddenly alone—backstage and aware only that the auditorium was quiet. *Empty? Had they all gone?*

I felt a calm presence behind me—taking my shoulders—gently leading me. Carly. She pulled back the curtain to show me that they were all still there—stunned silent by my abrupt exit—stunned silent and standing—every last one of them.

Carly nudged me out onto the stage. As I teetered near the edge with the white-hot stage lights blinding me, I heard myself saying—telling them, "*Sorry*— sorry about that."

I found my stool and sat. They sat too.

"I told you I'm new to this. It's just—that's all I had—all the songs I have." I looked down at the guitar in my lap searching for something more to say. I said, "A very dear friend of mine once shared with me her words to live by. *Good Friends, Full Hearts, Time of our Lives.* And I think that's how I feel tonight—about you, about all of this. Thank you—*for this*—for tonight."

*Applause.*

"I guess we can do one more—that be okay with you?"

*Thundering applause.*

"Yeah?—okay then." I cleared my throat. "Jackson wrote this song when he was sixteen."

*Clapping.*

"Yeah—*sixteen*. When I was sixteen, I couldn't be trusted to take out the trash. Anyway—Jackson's song of sixteen—for you—with a full heart—here is 'These Days.'"

Again, Jackson's lyrics seemed to sum me up. I'd spent the better part of this last year out walking and not doing much talking. Days spent thinking about loss and the things I didn't do, somehow afraid to live this life I'd made in song.

I SAT OFF STAGE, alone, watching as the stagehands took away Jackson's piano. Carly appeared and handed me a jumbo-sized bag of Lays chips.

"What's this?"

"Jackson sent instructions that these were to go to you."

I laughed, remembering his stash above Leah's fridge.

"You gonna share the joke?" she asked.

"Huh?"

"The chips," she said, "I'm guessing there's a joke in there somewhere. You know—do a show, get laid—have a good lay—something *rock star* like that?"

"Oh, right," I said. "No—nothing like that. It's just a secret indulgence of his—Jackson's—something he hides from his veggie-blender girlfriend."

"I see," she said, not totally buying it. "Well, if those chips don't do it for ya, the gang's gonna grab a bite around the corner where the shakshuka is out of this world."

"Sha-whatta?"

"Shakshuka—a spicy Tunisian stew with poached eggs."

I made a face which prompted her to assure me that I'd love it. Listening to her voice, I was inclined to believe I'd love anything she did.

She pulled an envelope from her jeans pocket. "Oh—almost forgot—nobody came—for the will call ticket. Sorry. Thought you should know."

I looked away.

"Someone special?" she asked.

"My dad," I told her.

"Sorry," she said again, "—he missed a good one."

I looked at her and she at me.

"Shakshuka," I said, "I accept."

"Yeah?" her eyes smiled, "—best."

THE GIRL HUNG CLOSE by my side, brushing back her white hair and smiling sweetly at me as we tripped along with the group to a place called Milk and Honey.

*Carly*, I thought to myself. The girl who took me by the sleeve and pulled me in.

I didn't go back to the hotel that night. I didn't walk alone those sinister streets—past what shadowy doom the supreme brotherhood may have arranged for me.

My life was to take a different course—one all my own.

## NBC STUDIOS/NEW YORK, NEW YORK

In the show's inaugural season, *Saturday Night Live* producer and creator, Lorne Michaels, spoke directly into the camera to share how the Beatles affected his life and the lives of his generation.

"In my book, the Beatles are the best thing that ever happened to music. It goes even deeper than that—you're not just a musical group, you're part of us. We grew up with you."

Then, reflecting the satire the show would come to be known for, Lorne Michaels delivered an offer to the band.

"Now, we've heard and read a lot about personality and legal conflicts that might prevent you guys from reuniting. That's something which is none of my business. That's a personal problem. You guys will have to handle that. But it's also been said that no one has yet to come up with enough money to satisfy you. Well, if it's money you want, there's no problem here. The National Broadcasting Company has authorized me to offer you this check to be on our show—a certified check for $3,000." He went on, "All you have to do is sing three Beatles songs. *She loves you, yeah, yeah, yeah*. That's a $1,000 right there. You know the words. It'll be easy. Like I said, this is made out to the Beatles. You divide it any way you want. If you want to give Ringo less, that's up to you."

Not a mile and a half away, John sat with an old friend in he and Yoko's New York apartment. Paul McCartney was in town promoting his Wings number one single, "Silly Love Songs", and had dropped in unannounced on John. It'd been years since the two of them were in the same room together.

John took Paul's visit as circumspect given he'd received an unexpected post just the day before. The package arrived without a note or return address. The post stamp read Portland, Oregon. John felt an uneasy clairvoyance about the package and for that reason, did not open it upon delivery.

He and Paul shared tea and toast points in front of the television serendipitously catching the SNL segment and Michaels' offer. "We nearly got into a cab and went down to the studio—just as a gag," John said later. Paul confirmed the episode adding, "We thought about it, going down and taking the money. But it would have been work, and we were having the night off."

Despite the two friends getting on, John would wait until

after Paul had left to retrieve the package and open it.

As Paul was leaving John said to him, "Think about me every now and then, old friend."

---

Source: Lorne Michaels excerpts taken from an inaugural season *Saturday Night Live* telecast on NBC.

# TWO YEARS LATER

## THE DAKOTA APARTMENTS/NEW YORK CITY/DECEMBER 8, 1980

Outside the arched entry of the Dakota building, the doorman, Jose Perdomo, put his back to the entrance and hunched over a clandestine cigarette. It was late and he leaned heavy on the stretch of quiet, the building's residents long retired on that chilly December night.

Across the archway, Perdomo took an uninterested glance at a solitary figure—a pudgy young man who had been skulking nearby for most of the afternoon and evening. Hearing voices, Perdomo dropped the lit butt and extinguished its remaining life beneath the sole of his shoe. He straightened up, pulling back his shoulders, then relaxed when he saw it was John and Yoko approaching.

Perdomo prepared to reach for the door handle, but hesitated when he saw John slow his stride and nod at the young man. John, too, apparently recognized the guy as the same autograph seeker from earlier. Something told John to keep moving though, and he did so with an arm full of tapes and Yoko at his side.

Perdomo reached a second time to open the door when a blast took out a window just above his head. He turned back to see the young man crouched in a military combat stance—his pistol aimed at John's back. Four shrill pops cut through the corridor, echoing off the brick and stone.

Lennon staggered toward the steps and stumbled into the lobby saying, "I'm shot, I'm shot." The cassette tapes he was holding scattered across the travertine floor where he fell face down. The concierge ran to him, saw the blood and damage. He removed his uniform blazer and placed it over the leaking holes in Lennon's back. He gently removed the broken, bloodied glasses from Lennon's face and summoned the police.

Still outside, Perdomo screamed at the shooter, "Do you know what you've done?" The shooter replied calmly, "Yes, I shot John Lennon."

The first team of police arrived to find the shooter standing against the building, stripped of his coat, the .38 revolver lying just yards away on the sidewalk. He was casually reading from a book, a paperback copy of J.D. Salinger's *Catcher In The Rye*.

Inside, a second team of officers knelt beside Lennon where a screaming Yoko cradled her husband's head. Determining it best to not wait for an ambulance, the officers lifted John into the backseat of their squad car. There, an Officer Moran asked him if he was John Lennon. John reportedly nodded and through a blood-filled mouth gurgled his final word, "Yes."

Three years later, Yoko Ono released posthumously John Lennon's final album titled, *Milk and Honey*.

---

## AUTHOR'S NOTE

I didn't choose to write this implausible story. The story chose me. The idea came to me after a work friend expounded on Steven King's novel, *11/22/63*, about a time traveler who tries to stop the JFK assassination. In *Golden Slumbers*, the fantastical device of the sunglasses giving rise to voyeuristic dreams both crystalized and perhaps doomed the story's implausible heart. That is until I stumbled upon instance after instance within the lyrics and lore of the Beatles that seem to support such a theory and thus make the implausible become plausible—even believable.

After all, it's easy to think of the Beatles as magical. Is it not?